COURIER

ZOE ROSI

LIGHTHOUSE
— BOOKS —

Cover design ©2024 Cong Nguyen

Published by Lighthouse Books, United Kingdom.

978-1-7384976-1-4

CHAPTER ONE

I've always hated delivering to 19 Samuel Close.

Nearly every time I've dropped off a package, I've heard shouting. Proper shouting.

It puts me off ringing the doorbell. I just leave deliveries by the door and hurry back to my van.

I try not to think about it, but I've found myself wondering who lives there. And yet I only seem able to conjure stereotypes, typical thug castings, grizzled and overbearing. Some sweaty, boozy bloke in a wife-beater vest with scuffed fists. Hardly original.

I don't know why I even give it any thought. It's not like it's got anything to do with me. I deliver hundreds of packages a day and a lot of the recipients are strange. Odd characters. Their lives are not my problem.

But today, I realised that 19 Samuel Close was on my route and the package was age-restricted, most likely alcohol, meaning it would have to be signed for, and the prospect has made me far more nervous than it probably should do.

I mean, I'm a 50-year-old man. I'm six foot two. I weigh fourteen and a half stone. I'm not generally easily intimidated.

But I suppose no one's immune to anxiety, and I've certainly felt it growing as I've been driving across town, ticking off deliveries, leaving 19 until last.

It doesn't help that the weather is on-the-nose atmospheric, all heavy clouds and scraggly trees, crude sketches against the sky. I've even spotted half a dozen crows, squawking aggressively, as though warning me of something. Or maybe I'm getting carried away.

I have one stop to go. One last delivery until I can't put this off any longer.

I get out of my van, keeping my head down from the drizzle drifting on the air, and get the package from the back. A large box, but light, probably containing something tiny swaddled in a lifetime's supply of cardboard. God help the trees. I buzz the intercom of a block of flats.

A woman buzzes me up, her voice tremulous, elderly.

There's no lift in the building, and of course, the flat is on the top floor.

By the time I've climbed up to the eighth floor and I'm knocking at the door, I'm out of breath and fairly pissed off.

Elderly customers tend to be the nicest, the most humane, still rooted in an era in which interactions were personal and people mattered, but the woman opens the door, clocks the package, grabs it without a word, without even glancing my way.

She shuts the door in my face, and I stand there for a moment, wheezing on her fucking doormat that says 'welcome' across it, and I have a maniacal urge to scream, to laugh hysterically, to kick the door, to bark like a fucking dog or screech like a hyena. Just to be noticed.

But I don't. Of course, I don't.

I just pick my non-existent pride up off the floor and head back downstairs.

Sometimes I think the day they replace us all with drones can't come soon enough. People are so fucking soulless. They get so wrapped up in their online shopping – browsing, clicking, scrolling – that they forget that the final part of their purchase – the delivery, actually involves a real person. A human being, with thoughts, emotions, feelings. They want us to be as anonymous as possible. As simple and forgettable as a click.

I leave the building and head back to my van.

Samuel Close is on my way home and as I make my way there, I think about what I'll do after. Dinner, maybe that fish pie in the freezer with peas. I've run out of wine. I could pick some up, but it is only Monday. Maybe I'll have a bath, read my book.

I put the radio on, but the *Radio Three* classics I usually quite like go right over my head.

Making my way from Saint Leonards, I head down Old London Road, by the seafront. The tide's in, frothing and curling. The beach is deserted.

Thoughts about dinner haven't quite cut it. I'm still nervous, I can't deny it. Nervous about

4

delivering a package! Ridiculous. But I've always had a nervous disposition. My grandmother used to call me a 'sensitive soul', her lips pursed and tight, as though she were choosing her words carefully, trying to be delicate about some awful affliction.

My dad was the same. To him, I was a 'wuss', a 'sissy'. It might have been different if I'd been into football, or if I hadn't been pushing fourteen by the time my voice broke. I'd started to think something was seriously wrong with me. That I might have some real-life Peter Pan condition and would stay squeaky-voiced and childlike forever.

The traffic lights by The White Rock Hotel are red. I wait, watching as a young girl crosses the road. A teenager, pushing a buggy, squawking into her phone, gold hoop earrings as big as the moon.

Sighing, I head up the hill towards Ore.

It still baffles me that I've ended up here.

Four years at university. A literature degree and a masters in Shakespeare from Durham – a bookish heyday in which I reinvented myself from awkward geek to well-read enigma, imagining a starry future in which I'd be the next F Scott. And here I am, a courier in a dead-end town. It would be funny if it weren't so tragic.

I followed my course mates to London, as was the done thing, but everyone was so boring there. As though the dreamy, free spirits they'd been at university had all been role play, a stepping stone before realising their true potential as corporate drones.

I couldn't get London to work for me. I switched between jobs, *so* many jobs, girlfriends, and uncomfortable house shares. Looking for something that fit, something that worked. I even travelled a bit, going on a few far-flung jaunts, but eventually, exhausted at thirty-three, I came here, to Hastings.

Hastings with its pier, its arcade, its miniature golf course, its ramshackle seafront Victoriana. Hastings with its old tumbling castle and steam train, its pound shops and council blocks and long-standing deprivation.

They have a name for people like me, locally: FILTH. Failed in London, trying Hastings.

I couldn't help but laugh the first time I heard it, it was just so true. Jaded Londoners come here all the time, looking for something different, something cheaper, something more bohemian, less intense. But most leave when the weather changes. They find they can't hack the bleak, harsh winters and they scarper back to the city.

It's a bit run down and parochial here compared to London. And yet, I've never quite been able to leave. I found I liked the pearlescent reflections of sunsets on wet sand when the tide's out. I liked the shabby, quiet, forgotten feel of the town. There's a certain peace, a much-needed stillness, to living in a nowhere place.

Sometimes I wonder if I've been hit by the curse of Crowley. It probably tells you all you need to know about Hastings that its most famous resident was an occultist. Aleister Crowley is said to have cursed the place, so that anyone who's ever lived here can never truly leave. They'll always end up coming back. The only way to break the curse is to find a pebble on the beach with a hole in it and take that with you the next time you try to break free.

I've never found such a stone, and more importantly, I've never looked.

I guess I'm happy enough here. This strange little place has suited me. I even had a shop for a while. Bob's Bazaar, in Old Town. Took on the lease from a mate down the pub – Nigel, a Saint Leonards Del Boy, affable in a vintage, cigar-chuffing way.

The shop wasn't much more than a laugh, a dare. A Carling-fuelled social experiment.

It sold all sorts: crystals, candles, dreamcatchers, sticks of rock, buckets and spades, snow globes, fridge magnets, postcards, handmade soaps, an esoteric collection of dog-eared second-hand books.

Strangely enough, it was a hit. Kids went wild for it, particularly the joke corner with its whoopee cushions, fake bugs, itching powder. God, they loved that stuff. But their parents seemed to like the place too, as though they couldn't get overpriced crystals and artisanal soap back home.

I'd sit behind the counter, all floppy hair and glasses, generally slightly sozzled from the bottle of Pinot Noir I tended to polish off steadily throughout the day, and I was the type of character a younger version of myself would probably have smirked at. Bob from Bob's Bazaar, a seaside oddity.

But I was fond of my shop. And I was gutted, really gutted, when after ten years, Nigel decided to hike the rent and turn it into an office space for the estate agent next door.

Ever since then, I've been sort of lost, adrift. It's a bit sad really, but it's true. I did odd jobs here and there: bar shifts, handyman stuff, upcycling furniture. I even tried to be an artist, creating low-rate wannabe Klimts, most of which ended up at the dump. And now, well, now I'm a courier.

A courier driving to the house of a man with a vile temper, whose name, by the way, is Nathaniel Sutherland, according to the labels on his packages.

Maybe I should have googled him.

I arrive outside the house and turn off the radio.

It's a beige, detached new build. Gleaming Range Rover in the driveway. Lawn trimmed to the point it looks like AstroTurf. One of twenty other identical houses. Very up-and-coming, nouveau riche.

I get out of my van. The drizzle's eased off now, but the sky's still murky, overcast. I get the package from the back.

Someone's dog's barking, a street or so away, as I cross the drive, glancing at the front room. Net curtains. No signs of life. No shouting, yet.

I ring the doorbell.

It chimes, and then silence.

Silence. Silence...

I contemplate pressing the bell again, or turning around, heading back, and then I hear something... Movement, footsteps down the hall.

He's coming.

The door opens and a man appears. He's not what I expected.

He's good-looking, stereotypically so. He's preened, a pretty boy. Ten years too old to be in Love Island, but the same sort of look. Ralph Lauren rugby shirt, pronounced pectorals, fade cut. Watch on display – chunky, probably low-rate designer. He's tanned too, in November! A sort of Donald Trump tan, totally over-baked. His eyebrows are more manicured than most women's.

'Alright, mate?' he says, with a smile, whitened teeth on full display.

It's a genuine smile though. Eyes sparkling and all.

He's friendly, warm even. It's the nicest, most humane greeting I've had all day. Most people, like that old bat from the last place, barely even look at me.

On good days, I tell myself my invisibility is okay. After all, it's not like I take any particular pride in being a courier. It doesn't mean anything to me. And I keep things deliberately low-key, with black sunglasses, a beanie hat, a long dark coat. I'm almost like a knock-off, less cool version of Morpheus from *The Matrix*. I could be anyone.

'You got something for me?'

That voice. Weirdly familiar, yet uncharacteristically calm.

I look down at the package I'm holding, a beat too slow, moronic.

'Need your date of birth,' I tell him. 'I have to enter it into the system.'

'Sure.' He tells me his date of birth as I punch it in. Turns out he's a Taurus. Typical.

11

'I need a signature too,' I say, handing over my signature pad.

He takes the electronic pen and does a squiggle as a girl pads barefoot into the hallway behind him. A little girl, maybe five or six.

She regards me nervously. She looks cowed, scared. There are unnatural shadows under her young eyes.

Nathaniel hands my signature pad back to me and reaches for his package as another figure appears down the hall. A young woman. Mid-twenties, perhaps. Her look is ethereal, sort of Snow White-like, with dark hair and big blue eyes. She's beautiful, and yet she's pale and meek, and there's a pleading, almost desperate look in her eyes.

'Cheers, mate.' Nathaniel clears his throat pointedly as he takes the package, as though wondering why I've not gone already.

Then he turns, following my gaze.

'Get back,' he hisses in that tone. That tone. There it is, the one I've heard him use before. I'm not sure whether he's speaking to the woman or the kid, but both scarper.

He closes the door.

I stand on the doorstep for a moment, wanting to do something. Help that woman, that child. But what can I do?

I stare at the red painted door and then turn around and head back to my van.

.

CHAPTER TWO

I try to lose myself in the pages of *The Mahābhārata*, which I've been trying to get into for a while now, but I can't help finding it a bit dense, a bit soporific.

Usually, I love my spiritual texts. Nothing beats *The Upanishads*, but really, I'm a bit of a spirituality whore. I'll read anything: *The Bible*, *The Koran*, *The Talmud*, the writings of Baha'u'llah, Bhagavad Gita, *The Tibetan Book of the Dead*. Anything that promises some form of enlightenment or enrichment, I guess.

But I find myself putting my book down and going online. Nathaniel's intriguing me more than Indian epics tonight. I should forget about him and his twisted life, but my curiosity gets the better of me.

It doesn't take long to find his Instagram page. You'd think he'd go by Nathan, but no. Nathaniel, apparently.

He's a personal trainer, or at least that's what he claims. His bio contains a link leading to an, 'Oops. This page can't be found' result. Impressive.

I scroll through his pictures. Flexing mirror shots. Glossy, oiled up abs. Barbell posturing. Pouting car selfies. Pure narcissism. He supports Manchester United and considers it his defining personality trait. There are shots of him and his mates at the pub, brandishing Man United scarves like banners, pint glasses everywhere.

I think of my father. They'd have got along well.

There's not a single photo with that woman, his partner presumably, or of his kid. To all intents and purposes, Nathaniel looks like a single man.

I find myself needing to know more. To see that woman's face again. I can't seem to dispel the urge. I check Facebook, but surprisingly Nathaniel isn't on there. His only online presence appears to be his Instagram account and a handful of Google reviews he's offered up. Finds the chicken wings at Chick 'n' Chips a bit too soft, apparently. But happens to really like his local Chinese.

I *need* to know that woman's name. I type into Google, 'how to find names of residents at address', and, as it turns out, it's surprisingly easy to get the information. There's a site that allows me to run an electoral roll search, which reveals that there are two adults living at 19 Samuel Close: Nathaniel and Natalie Sutherland, both of whom have resided at the property for six years. Naturally, the child isn't included on the electoral roll.

Unlike Nathaniel, Natalie Sutherland is on Facebook, although her profile – *your* profile – is irritatingly locked down.

Only three pictures on show to the public and nothing more. Just three pictures showcasing your beauty, because you, Natalie, are beautiful.

When you're not scared and pale and shaken, you glow. You're vibrant, with sparkling eyes, a wide, dimpled smile, flawless skin, dark, glossy hair.

My heartrate quickens as I click back and forth through your pictures, unable to quite believe it. You're heaven. *Heaven.*

What are you doing with Nathaniel? You're in a different league.

There's none of that duck lip, Botox, filler stuff with you. That weird plastic look that makes every person who subscribes to it look vaguely related. Members of some grotesque extended family.

No, your beauty is real. It's real and powerful, rare.

And it's as though you don't even know it. You're all lashes and doe eyes and tentative, bashful smiles. No posturing, no posing, no showing off. No filters, no angles. Not like Nathaniel.

To think that monster's keeping you – a treasure, a princess – trapped in his poor man's excuse for a castle. Shouting at you. Screaming at you. It's a fucking disgrace.

There's a shot of you in your garden, your beige home behind you, smiling shyly by a flowerbed.

Another of you, sitting on the sofa, your arms around that little girl's shoulders. Clearly your daughter. You look alike, up close. She has your eyes, your gorgeous eyes. She's smiling, laughing. She's not afraid here, in your arms. Not like earlier.

My heart aches.

The third shot is of you by the sea, on a bright, wintry day. Your windswept hair blows across your face, and the light picks out faint shadows under your eyes, but weirdly, they make you look more attractive. Touching. Fragile. You smile as though your smile's an accident, a mishap, and you shouldn't be smiling at all. I bet Nathaniel took this one.

That's what he's done to you, that insecurity, that sadness. It makes me want to wrap you up in cotton wool, tell you you're beautiful, never let anyone hurt you again.

I don't know how many times I flick back and forth through these pictures, Natalie. These three beautiful pictures.

I screenshot them and save them on my phone. They're the last thing I look at before I go to sleep.

I imagine what your voice sounds like. What you smell like. How your touch would feel.

CHAPTER THREE

It might sound strange, but I start driving past your house at the start of my shift and at the end. Just to catch a glimpse of you.

But I don't think he lets you out, Natalie.

I must have driven by a dozen times. Sometimes I linger. I park at the end of your road and hang about, waiting to see you, but I never do.

It's not right.

I watched for the whole day last Thursday. I had the day off and I parked where your road turns off onto Alexandra Parade. I sat there for hours, like an undercover cop. I thought I might start to look conspicuous, but no one pays delivery vans much attention. I guess that cloak of courier invisibility comes in handy sometimes.

I sat reading my book, an old classic this time – can't beat *The Tripitaka* – while keeping an eye on your house. I watched and I waited. Nathaniel came out at 12.35pm, gym bag over his shoulder, key fob pointed at his flashing car.

He has a swagger to the way he walks, doesn't he? As though he commands attention, even though the street was perfectly quiet, and no one was looking his way. Well, no one but me.

He got in his car and pulled out of the drive. I kept my head down as he came down the road.

What do you see in him, Natalie? Surely, it's not just his muscles, those pecs that stretch his top like shrink-wrapping. You're better than that. You deserve better than that.

I sit there, knowing he's gone and you're alone. I'm tempted to grab a package, one of the stray ones in the back of my van, just so I can go and knock on your door, pretend I've got the wrong house, see you up close. Lock eyes with you. See you bat your lashes.

The thought is weirdly arousing, acutely arousing actually, and I find myself clambering into the back of the van.

I imagine you letting me in, pleading with me to save you, save you from him. Begging me, pawing at me, kissing me. The fantasy unfolds in my mind and my dick is solid, rock solid.

I pleasure myself and come hard into an old McDonald's carton. Not my finest moment, I'll admit, but it did feel good.

I do that a few times, actually. Shameful, I know, I know. But you do something to me, Natalie. You're just so... You're just so *you*.

It's borderline merciful when Nathaniel finally reappears, at 2.40pm. A long gym session. He still looks fresh as a daisy, hair gelled to perfection, obviously having preened himself in the changing rooms. He swaggers back inside.

He's not a personal trainer, is he, Natalie? He just goes to the gym. How's he supporting you? Are you okay?

There's not another peep from your house. I should go, really. But I end up waiting until around 10pm, when the street's enveloped in darkness, and I can't face any more of *The Tripitaka*. I've eaten all the Greggs supplies I brought with me and pissed twice down a nearby alleyway. My eyelids are drooping, and I don't think I can stay awake much longer.

I know what I needed to know. I've confirmed what I suspected. Nathaniel's keeping you in that house like a prisoner, a hostage, a possession.

And frankly... Well, frankly, it's a crime.

It's a crime that he's holing you up: trapping you, shouting at you, isolating you from everyone and everything. Denying you the world, and denying the world, you. You deserve to be free. You deserve to be beautifully, spectacularly free.

It's your birthright. It's your destiny. It's the very fucking least you deserve.

It's the very fucking least any of us deserve.

CHAPTER FOUR

I know it's strange, but I deliver my parcels and go about my routine, just like before, and yet I can't stop thinking about you. It's as though there's this thread between us, a cord. I think of you, the way you stood in the hallway behind Nathaniel. A broken doll, a marionette, a deer in the headlights. Face washed out and sad. Did you appear that day for a reason? Was it some sort of cry for help? Did you sense something in me?

Probably not. Of course not. But I think about that moment. You, ghostly and pale and pleading, just before Nathaniel closed the door.

You looked slighter than you do in your pictures.

I worry about you, Natalie.

I try to tell myself not to get invested, that it's none of my business. Your problems and your relationship are nothing to do with me. This fixation I have, this interest, it's not normal. It's not healthy. I don't know you, you're just a stranger. I shouldn't get involved.

And yet, I can't seem to shake you. I can't seem to let you go. I know how that monster, that animal, that pathetic excuse of a man, speaks to you and your daughter, and I'm worried.

I need to know you're okay, that's all. I'll keep an eye on you for a bit, just to make sure, and then I'll leave it. I'll leave it and forget all about you.

I'll delete the pictures of you from my phone. Permanently. Go back to my deliveries, go back to minding my own business.

CHAPTER FIVE

I got so close to your house tonight Natalie that my left cheek was flush against its cool brick.

It was surprisingly easy to get so close and it thrilled me, it really did.

There's a field at the back of your garden. I scoped the area out, climbed over the fence around the field's edge and had a wander, as though I were an intrepid walker enjoying a cheeky jaunt.

Your garden fence is around my height, which isn't ideal. And it's sturdy too. Annoyingly so. I tested each panel, inspecting the joinery. But it was secure, sealed, bonded with industrial glue. Since when has new build construction been this good?

But I figured there must be a way around it. I'm no quitter.

I double-checked the panels, and then my foot sank into a dip in the soil, a burrow made by some animal, and I got an idea. I could go *under*. Burrow my way to you.

So I went and bought a small shovel and once it got dark, I came back. I dug, bit by bit, until there was a gap big enough for me to slide under like a worm. I pictured you and Nathaniel watching TV inside while I was out back, slithering in the darkness.

It's weird, Natalie, I know, but forgive me these transgressions. I've had to go to some extreme lengths because these are extreme circumstances.

Slipping under your fence, I crept in the darkness across your surprisingly long garden until I arrived at the back of your house, gasping with relief, like some sort of army commando returning to base.

I could see into your kitchen, flawless. Not a stray plate. Not a speck of dirt. Like something from a catalogue. It didn't look lived in at all. There was something unsettling, suffocating, about its show home look. I bet Nathaniel screams that standard into you.

I waited a while, crouching by your back wall, wondering what I was doing, contemplating going home, and then I saw a shadow move across the window. A woman's shadow.

You.

You!

And then the sound of gushing, water down a drain, a running tap. Were you doing the washing up?

That's when I pressed my face against the wall, Natalie. We were so close. So very close! Just a few feet between us.

I closed my eyes, smiled.

And then *he* came along and ruined *everything*. He's disgusting, Natalie. The way he speaks to you, the things he says. I won't repeat them. I'm better than that, and you know them all too well. That bastard's had more than enough airtime already. Far more than enough.

Why do you put up with it, Natalie? Why do you stay with him? Is it because of your daughter? How do you cope?

I wanted to smash my way into the kitchen, straight through the glass-panelled back doors, and punch that prick's fucking lights out.

But I clenched and unclenched my fists in the darkness instead, tears pricking at my eyes.

Then the kitchen light went off, a door slammed, and everything went quiet. One by one, all the lights went off.

I waited a bit. Then, I slunk back across the garden, slipped under the fence, refilled the hole. I packed the dirt down, gritting my teeth.

I went home feeling horrible and grubby, but not because of the soil clinging to my clothes.

CHAPTER SIX

I have another confession to make Natalie.

I've been trying to befriend you on Facebook. You can't really expect me to be content with just those three pictures, can you?

They tantalised me, whet my appetite, but I couldn't just stop there.

I'm not on Facebook myself, that kind of thing's not for me. I prefer talking to people, looking into their eyes, having a real connection, not hitting 'like' on a picture or tapping out some half-hearted comment. That's not my style and I've never had a single social media profile. Not one.

I suppose I could have created one, started a Facebook account for the sole purpose of befriending you, but I didn't want the first time we 'meet' to be so two dimensional, so uninspiring.

It's going to be different. Special.

So I decided to knock up a fake profile, to catfish you. I know it's not nice to deceive you, Natalie, but there are worse things a person can do. I just want to look, is that really so bad?

I find a young woman from Kentucky. Your average blonde: plump, smiley, a bit dumb looking. I nick a dozen of her pictures and then block her.

I christen myself Kayla Samuels and upload the photos, adding a simpleton's bio, a sort of ChatGPT-generated spiel for an idiot. All 'nights in with my fella, bopping along to Ariana Grande, cocktails with the girlies' kind of crap. I add a few spelling mistakes to make it look even more authentic.

I can't request your friendship straight away when I don't have any other friends. That would be weird. So over a couple of days, I add hundreds of people, hundreds, figuring at least some of them will accept a friend request from a sweet-looking blonde.

It works. Sixty-five people accept, and then I add you.

Request pending.

For five days, Natalie? Five days! I mean, come on.

I check again and my request has been cancelled. Natalie!

So you weren't interested in being friends with Kayla. I suppose it's fair enough. It's not like you know her.

I swear a few times, though. Groan into the nothingness of my flat, and then I try again.

This time, I take a different approach.

I find pictures of a man, an attractive man. Around your age.

He looks a bit like that guy in One Direction. Zayn Malik, I believe. All tattoos and earrings and dark, brooding eyes. He's a painter, apparently. Lives in Brooklyn. A popular character, by the looks of it. Four thousand, three hundred and thirty-eight friends.

I save a bunch of his pictures – he takes a *lot* of selfies. Then I block him and create a new profile. This time I'm Dan Reid. A student, from Hackney, London.

I go through the same routine of adding friends, only even more intensely. I add thousands of people over the course of three days, and eventually Dan ends up with two hundred and seventy-four.

I know what I'm doing is pathetic, Natalie, I know. In a way, I'm proving a point about the hollowness of social media, aren't I...? I just want to look at your page, Natalie. Just a bit.

I add some posts to Dan's page, musings about pop culture, his selfies, generic crap. I don't want you being *too* impressed by him.

And then I add you.

Half an hour later, you accept. Really, Natalie?!

I'm not sure quite how to feel about that.

Should I be jealous or is this a good thing? Is your openness towards Dan a sign that you're losing interest in Nathaniel?

I decide to go with the latter interpretation.

The most important thing is that I now have access to your profile. At last! A veritable treasure trove of *you.*

I'm giddy with it, hardly breathing, as I scroll through your pictures like a maniac. Gulping up your videos, because you post them. Videos! Just little ones, like you a few years ago in a Santa hat wishing everyone a happy Christmas, blowing a kiss. Normally, I'd find that kind of thing tacky, but with you it's somehow adorable. And your voice. Your voice... It's beautiful. Musical. Deeper than I thought it would be. Sexy. Oh, Natalie!

I scroll and scroll. Reading every single thing you've ever posted, right back until you joined in June 2013. At this point, the sun's coming up outside and I've barely torn my eyes from the screen. I'm not even tired, Natalie.

You're more than I could ever have imagined. You're perfect.

I knew my feeling about you was right. I knew you were special.

We're different, but I like it.

You're not into books or culture or spirituality. You're not ambitious. You don't dream of being great, exceptional, different. You don't waste your energy on fantasies of literary stardom, like I did. You're better than that. You're content with the little things, with normality. I'd have saved myself so much anguish if I'd only been like you.

You're a bit of a Facebook hun. You post about TV shows, cakes you've baked, new clothes, inspirational quotes (which normally I'd find a turn-off, but with you, are kind of cute), and your daughter, Cara. You post about her a lot. Photos (baby pictures, first day at school, shots of her doing finger painting, making daisy chains, etcetera). You love her, dearly.

There's not a lot about Nathaniel. Apart from a few early pictures of you two back when you were teenagers. Nathaniel had an eyebrow piercing back then and was spotty and greasy looking. Turns out you're childhood sweethearts.

Is that why you put up with him, Natalie? Some kind of deep-seated loyalty?

I click and click, and find one picture, in which you've dubbed yourselves 'the Natsters'.

The Natsters.

Natalie...

I must really like you, because not even that puts me off.

Okay, it's not exactly selling you, but it's not putting me off, and that's something.

The Natsters. Even your friends called you that.

Becky Gilbert: *The Natsters are looking GOOOOD!*

There's one shot of you two snogging in the corner of a party. It's intimate. You're sitting on the kitchen counter, your legs wrapped around Nathaniel's hips.

One of your friends – Tommy Mathias – has commented: '*Get a room, Natsters*', and I have to say, I agree.

The Natsters. Honestly!

But I suppose I did some dodgy things when I was younger. Nothing like this, but not great either.

I feel a bit defeated though as I look at these snaps, taking in your young, unselfconscious, grinning faces. You both looked so happy back then. Bright-eyed and bushy-tailed.

Although there's one picture that's a bit different to the rest. A shot of Nathaniel, smiling at a dinner table, Sunday roast before him, looking less keyed up than in the other shots. You've written an intriguing caption.

So proud of my love. Three months sober. No booze and no brown. Just cigs. This wasn't easy but you did it, babe.

No brown? So Nathaniel was a junkie?

Interesting...

I'm still feeling down though that this loser is your childhood sweetheart. Even a drug problem didn't put you off.

How can I compete with your longest relationship? Possibly your *only* relationship?

Sure, I want to get between you two. Let's not pretend that hasn't been the idea all along, but *childhood sweethearts.* There's something unsettling about that. That level of connectedness. I can't even begin to relate to it.

There are a few shots from your wedding, too. From September 2016. No offence, Natalie, but it looks pretty tacky. Is that a community centre, some kind of *bingo hall?* It looks like the kind of place that would smell. And your dress. It's just... flammable.

You're stunning, Natalie. Come on. You deserve better than that.

I click right through the handful of shots on display. They're distasteful.

Needing a break, I head to the kitchen and pour myself a generous glass of Shiraz. A cheapish bottle from Tesco that's one of the few under-a-tenner brands I've found that doesn't have a tang.

Sitting back down at my laptop, I sip and scroll. The wine warms me, softening the edges of my dismay. By the time I'm refilling my glass, I'm feeling better, calmer.

So, you and Nathaniel go way back. You're childhood sweethearts. It's not ideal, of course it's not. But I try to see the positives.

Firstly, you don't post pictures of him anymore. At all.

There are none of Nathaniel on your page, none of you two together. Not for years.

Clearly, the Natsters aren't exactly going strong these days.

And secondly, I know this is bad, but if you've only ever known what life is like in a relationship, then if Nathaniel is no longer in the picture, you're going to struggle, really struggle, to be alone.

You're going to need someone.

And I could be there for you, Natalie. I could truly be there for you.

There's always a silver lining to every cloud, if you look closely enough. Or drink enough wine.

CHAPTER SEVEN

You're the first thing I think about when I wake up.

I click through your pictures. Scroll and scroll. But they're not quite hitting the spot.

I need more of you. Just a little more.

So I put on my shades, get in my van and head down to your road.

I park at the end and wait.

But you don't come out. Not even on a Saturday.

Surely, he doesn't keep you cooped up all weekend, Natalie?

You need to breathe, feel the sun on your skin. It's not healthy.

I listen to one of my favourite podcasts, *The Rising Sun Show*. It focuses on the law of attraction, manifestation, spiritual wellbeing, and normally I find its episodes quite engrossing. I'm a big fan of the host, Serena Soulful, whose teachings aren't anywhere near as tacky as her name. I've been into her stuff for a while now, ever since my job as a courier first started to make me feel erased. Serena gave me a sense of my own power, my autonomy. But it's hard to fully concentrate on the show when I have you on my mind.

I get through three episodes and start a fourth, and there's still nothing from your house. Not even Nathaniel comes out.

I'm hungry. I didn't bring any food with me and all I've eaten is a banana I had back at my flat.

My stomach rumbles and I'm close to heading home, or at least going to the corner shop for a bag of crisps, when at 4.15pm, you emerge. You, Nathaniel and Cara.

You!

You look tired, head down, shuffling. Almost as though you're afraid to look up, to engage with the world. You're dressed sportily, in bright colours that clash with your wan expression. Why are you looking so low, Natalie? What's he done? I want to get out of my van, go over, hug you.

You really are thinner than you are in your pictures. So much less happy. Oh God, I do worry about you, Natalie.

Your clothes look new, fresh. Have you ever worn them out before? Is that one of the things Nathaniel orders? Clothes for you?

You all pile into your car. There's an air of purposefulness about you, and I wonder where you're going.

A day trip? Shopping? Some sort of social thing?

I sit up straighter, tapping my fingers against the steering wheel. What's Nathaniel roped you into?

I turn my podcast off and twist my key in the ignition. I'll see where you're going, just to make sure you're okay.

Nathaniel drives right across Hastings. The streets are irritatingly busy, and I've never actually followed anyone before. I almost lose you, but I just about keep you in sight. Nathaniel joins the A259, heading west. Are you going to Bexhill?

I ransack my memories of your Facebook page for recollections of posts about Bexhill. Do you know people there?

The A259 isn't quite as busy and I hang back, letting a few cars slip between you and me.

Nathaniel passes Bexhill and goes even further west, towards Polegate. I start to wonder whether I should turn around. He could be going anywhere, after all. This is ridiculous. And yet, the thought's abstract in my mind, disconnected, and I know I'm not going back.

Then, Nathaniel turns off down Beachy Head Road.

I follow. There are no other vehicles between us now and I feel exposed. I'm half-worried Nathaniel might stop suddenly and confront me about following him. And yet, I sort of doubt he's that observant.

But I hang back as much as possible as you drive towards the cliffs and park in the car park.

I'm not sure how I feel about this. A family stroll along the most fatal cliff face in the country with a psychopath like Nathaniel. What if he loses it and pushes you off, and then calls it an accident? Did he bring you here to intimidate you? There are plenty of less daunting places for you to walk.

I park further down the road, tucking my van behind a tree. I'm far enough away that you can't see me, but close enough for me to keep an eye on you.

You get out of the car, head down, still forlorn. I don't blame you.

Nathaniel hops out too, all slamming doors and cockiness. Cara rushes towards you and grabs your hand.

You start walking towards the cliffs. I get out of my van. I don't like this. I don't like this at all. Something feels off.

I walk towards the cliffs too, alongside the gnarled brambles and crooked trees, bent permanently out of shape by the harsh winds of this brutal, exposed spot.

You're walking, ambling. You pass a couple strolling hand in hand, relaxed and intimate, unlike you and Nathaniel.

It's strange thinking of you seen through the eyes of strangers. You probably look like a regular young family. Aspirational, with your new clothes and your big car.

But strangers don't know what your life is really like. They don't know about the shouting, the rage, the abuse.

The couple pass, heading back to the car park, and it's just you, Nathaniel and Cara, alone in this beautiful, staggeringly dangerous place.

I've been here a handful of times before. It's further away than I usually venture, but the landscape suits a certain mood – a dark, troubled ennui. With its steep chalk cliffs, waves breaking soundlessly against the rocks far below, and foreboding signs dotted along the cliff face warning of the fatal drop. Unnerving, and yet a promise to many who've come here over the years. A reassurance.

The wind is buoyant. Not rough like it can be here, but it's whipping your hair up into the air. You reach up and tuck it back.

And then you turn, almost as if you've felt me looking. You glance my way.

Our eyes meet.

Or at least, I think they do.

I freeze, and my heart leaps into my mouth.

I shrink behind a bramble, turn rigid, look out to sea, barely breathing.

Did you see me?

I'm far enough away that surely, I wouldn't be much more than a smudge on the horizon. I've got my shades and hat on, too. I'm just a figure. A nobody.

I wait a few beats, peer around the bramble.

You've turned back. You didn't see me, not really. I'm too far away. I'm just a stranger, anyway.

But my heart's beating, pounding in my chest.

That felt close.

I sit down. I need a reprieve. I can't keep trailing you and risk exposure.

And anyway, even if Nathaniel did do something, I'm too far away to stop him. It's a horrific thought, but it's true. One push, one second would be all it would take in this fatal place. I just need to hope for the best, pray.

Please be okay, please, I silently urge as you retreat out of sight, further along the horizon.

I turn my attention to the view. The sea is choppy and the sun's beginning to set. It oozes rich orange sherbetty light across the sky. It's one of those sunsets where the light seems to have a life of its own; it's paint-like, fluid, and spills into the wispy clouds, turning them into ribbons of pink and gold.

It's stunning, truly stunning. And I consider it our first sunset. Because even if Nathaniel had his arm around you right now, I know you wouldn't really be there with him.

Does a brute like Nathaniel even have it in him to notice a sunset, even one as spectacular as this?

I doubt it. I'm surprised he even brought you here. He was either trying to scare you or he saw some reel on Instagram. Some stupid Z-list celebrity waxing lyrical about country walks, or maybe one of the Man United players he so looks up to.

'Excuse me.'

A man's voice. Behind me.

I turn, terrified, half-expecting it to be Nathaniel. But it's an older guy, mid-sixties, dressed for hiking. I breathe.

'Sorry to bother you. Are you local?'

He has a charming face. Led a nice life. You can just tell with some people.

'Yes,' I reply, my voice strained. I really thought I'd just been rumbled.

'Great!' He enthuses.

I smile awkwardly. I'm not even local, not really.

'Do you know any decent pubs nearby? We're not getting signal up here and, well, we're pretty hungry!'

He glances at his wife, who's standing behind him, as though shy.

As it happens, I do know a decent pub. It's pretty much the only pub around here and it is a good one. I had a roast dinner there once, a few years back.

I tell him about it, pointing, giving directions.

The man's grateful and thanks me heartily.

I beam back, oh so gracious, as he walks away.

As he and his partner retreat, I realise he's the first person I've spoken to for weeks, beyond the odd mumble when making a delivery. I'm slightly unnerved by the sound of my own voice, articulating full sentences, and my eyes, holding eye contact. I'd almost forgotten I could do that – be nice, normal. I feel bizarrely proud of myself. I can still pass as a regular person after all. I can still just about fit into society. I'm not just a nobody, a faceless courier.

I turn back to the sunset. It's even more lavish now, incredible.

The person I really want to rediscover conversation with is you, Natalie. I want us to talk for hours. I want to be the person I used to be back when I laughed, when I had fun, when I was silly.

It's been years since I was that person. It makes my skin prickle to think about it.

I look further along the cliffs, see some figures in the distance. Too far away to make out. Is that you?

The figures get closer. Two adults, a child. It is you. I recognise Nathaniel's walk. Your top.

You're gesticulating, both you and Nathaniel. You look like you're arguing.

I get up to head back to my van, keeping an eye on you. I had a bad feeling about this walk and now it looks like something's happened between you and that monster after all.

I creep back, staying close to the brambles. I get inside as you're approaching your car.

You're still gesticulating, wildly. You're upset, really upset, but Nathaniel... Nathaniel's *raging*. I'm a few hundred metres away and I can hear him shouting from here, catch a few of his words. Does he ever let up, Natalie?

Poor Cara is cowering behind you, head down. She deserves better than this.

The car flashes as Nathaniel unlocks it.

He pulls open the door to get inside, but you're hanging back, like you don't want to go with him. You're crying, shrinking away. He groans, loud enough for me to hear, and marches over to you. He raises his hand and whacks you, right across the head. You shriek, flinching, and he does it again, and you shriek again, cowering. He yanks open the passenger door and shoves you in, slamming the door closed.

Cara's wailing. Nathaniel turns and screams at her, grabbing her and stuffing her into the backseat like she's a doll.

Then, with both of you inside, he screams, just screams. He's deranged, utterly deranged.

He gets in the car. Jerkily, he reverses and pulls out of the car park, and then he's off, whizzing down the road, towards me.

I lower my head, keeping down. The car passes, a blur on my peripheral vision.

I feel it retreat, and silence return.

I raise my head. The sun has really exploded now, like lava, pouring everywhere. It's spectacular, one of the best sunsets I've seen in years, and yet so sad. You should be enjoying this. And yet you're crying, you're scared, you're stuck with *him*. What kind of world do we live in where a woman like you misses out on such a glorious sunset?

Tears prick my eyes. I blink them away and try not to think about how much I'm shaking.

CHAPTER EIGHT

I've never exactly been a fan of Aleister Crowley, but I do appreciate his motto, 'do as thou wilt shall be the way of the law', and suddenly it's become quite appealing.

I won't sit back while you get abused, Natalie. Sorry, but I just won't. I won't let him get away with it. I'm going to have to do something. Take matters into my own hands and save you. Do as I wilt.

I mean, would it be such a loss if something bad happened to Nathaniel? What's the point of a person like him. I mean, really? He's bringing nothing but misery to everyone around him, including himself. He's toxic, completely pointless.

He needs to go. He needs to be jettisoned into oblivion.

It's not like you're going to leave him anytime soon. No offence, Natalie. I get it, I do. You clearly have some form of Stockholm Syndrome.

Or Nathaniel's fucked with your head so badly that you actually believe you deserve abuse. Perhaps you think being whacked on a Saturday afternoon is somehow excusable rather than a genuine fucking atrocity. No, Natalie. I won't let you live like that. I won't let you accept that kind of bullshit. I won't have it. I won't let him turn you into a husk, a depository for all his pain and shame and self-hate. That's not the fate you deserve. I won't let him destroy you and Cara.

You need help.

And I'm going to help you, Natalie. I'm not quite sure how yet, but I'm going to intervene. Nathaniel won't be able to hurt you much longer. I'm going to make sure of that.

CHAPTER NINE

I should have anticipated that I'd have to deliver to you again. And yet somehow, I got so wrapped up in you that I almost forgot I'm your courier.

I see his name on my deliveries list. Nathaniel Sutherland. Age restricted once more. My stomach twists.

I could handle leaving packages on your doorstep, but interacting with Nathaniel? After what I saw yesterday?

For fuck's sake. The universe can be so fucking cruel.

I don't know how I'm going to keep my cool.

Or, worse, what if you answer? That's not how we're supposed to meet. I have other plans for us, Natalie. We can't meet when I'm delivering. That would be wrong, it would ruin everything.

I consider seeing if one of the guys at the depot will do the delivery for me. I could say I know someone at the house, make up a story about a crazy ex or something. But lying, and connecting myself to your address, doesn't feel like a good idea. So, I leave it.

Instead of putting the delivery off until the end of the day, like before, I decide to get it over with as soon as possible. There's no way I can go about my day with this at the back of my mind.

I'm dressed like every other day: black beanie hat, sunglasses, long coat. Guarded, disguised, nondescript.

Even if you did answer the door, would I register? Probably not.

I'm still not happy about the idea of it though, and for the first time, I *want* to see Nathaniel.

I park outside your house. Get the package from the back. It's rectangular, longish. I feel something rattling around inside. A bottle of booze, I think.

Skin crawling, stomach twisted, I cross your front drive and press the buzzer.

My heart's in my mouth as I hear footsteps down the hall.

Don't be you. Don't be you...

The door opens. It's him.

I smile. I actually smile!

Nathaniel looks like he's just woken up, in pyjamas, with messy hair and a dazed look.

'Need your date of birth for the package,' I say.

He grumbles, gives it to me. He doesn't seem to recognise me, not at all. I'm yet another courier.

'And a signature too, I'm afraid.' I present my signature pad.

Nathaniel smiles weakly and does a squiggle. I look over his shoulder, but the hallway's empty. I'm glad you're not there, Natalie, but I wonder where you are, what you're doing, if you're okay.

Nathaniel hands the pad back to me and takes the package.

'Thanks, dude,' he says, closing the door.

Thanks, dude? That makes me want to push the door back open and strangle him. What a fucking phoney. I know what he is, how he treats you.

Clenching my fists, still stuck on the doorstep, I remind myself that he's going to get what's coming.

Not right now, but soon enough.

'See you later, *dude*,' I reply to the closed door.

And then I breathe and go back to my van.

I get in and look back at your house, or should I call it your prison? I'm half-expecting you to be standing at one of the upstairs windows, forlorn and Rapunzel-like, hair trailing over the windowsill, but you're not there. The curtains are drawn.

I hope you're okay, Natalie. I really do.

I drive away. It takes a few more deliveries until my heart stops pounding.

I check Nathaniel's Instagram when I finally get home.

He's posted a story of him clutching a bottle of Ledaig, which, according to Google, is a fairly obscure Scottish whisky. He's written: '*Drinking in honour of my dad. His favourite tipple. Three years gone. RIP Pops.*'

Interesting.

Was that the bottle he ordered? It would make sense. You probably can't get Ledaig from Tesco.

I wonder how you feel about Nathaniel's boozing, Natalie?

I don't like the idea of him drunk. It doesn't sound safe. It doesn't sound safe at all.

Chapter Ten

I listen to a few episodes of *The Rising Sun Show* and something Serena Soulful says inspires me. A manifestation trick that involves writing a note to the universe.

I get a piece of my best writing paper – off-white, lightly textured – and my special quill, a peacock feather crafted to a perfect point. I dip my quill in black ink, as inky as the night's sky. Sitting at my kitchen table with a few candles lit, breathing deeply, my mind and body full of intention, I write a note.

Help me find a way to deal with Nathaniel.

Then I fold it up, concentrating, folding my intention into it.

I place the paper in a pot, which I'm now going to consider my manifestation pot. It's a hand-painted one I bought from a quirky little shop in

Brighton. I leave it by my bedroom window before I go to sleep, to soak up the light from the moon.

CHAPTER ELEVEN

You're staying with your sister.

You posted about it on Facebook a few days ago.

Nothing quite like having a week in Epping Forest with my sis. I need this!

Your caption was accompanied by a shot of a garden stretching into woodland. Nice.

The post is short and sweet by your standards, but it makes sense that you wouldn't want your Facebook friends to know what's been going on between you and Nathaniel, and the real reason you clearly need a break. It's hardly the wholesome family image you'd want the world to see.

It's promising that you've taken action though, Natalie. I'm proud of you. I'm glad you've removed yourself from Nathaniel, even if it isn't permanent.

What concerns me though, is that you've done this before. According to your posts, you went to stay with your sister under similarly vague circumstances in January 2017, again in November 2017, September 2018, twice in 2019 and so on. I guess what I'm trying to say is you do this a lot.

It seems your sister, Janine, offers a bit of a release valve for your relationship with Nathaniel. When things get unbearable between you two, you seek refuge at her place. And then what, Natalie? Nathaniel apologizes, buys you flowers, and you go back, try again?

Can't you see it's not working? How long are you going to live like this? Running off to Janine, then running back to him? What's it going to take for you to realise you deserve better?

What would it take for you to walk?

Sadly, I don't think you have it in you to do that. I hate to say that, Natalie, I really do. I'm not trying to be offensive, but you're too scared. You're too weak, too reliant on him. You don't have the confidence, Natalie. You don't have the fight.

I get it. He sunk his claws into you when you were young, too young to have developed your own strength.

But on some level, you must know you can't go on like this. Surely, you know that.

But don't worry, Natalie. I'm going to help. I'm going to take Nathaniel out of the picture. I'll set you free.

I have fantasies of strangling the fucker in the alleyway by the gym he frequents, but it's just a fantasy. I may be a bit taller than Nathaniel, but he's more muscular. A lot more, actually. It would be an awful fight, some ridiculous, messy punch-up, in which, let's face it, I'd probably lose. And that's not my style.

Something will come to me though, I know it. My manifestation pot will deliver.

A few days pass. Then, as I'm sorting packages at the depot, I find one for your place, another age-restricted package. It feels just like the last one, the one I believe contained that bottle of whisky, and I get an idea.

A bizarre idea, but it comes to me clearly and effortlessly, and there's something about it that just feels right, so I act on it immediately.

I deliver all my parcels as quickly as I can, and then I go back to my place, with the package for Nathaniel.

Inside my flat, I place it on the kitchen table.

How did I not think of this before?

This package is my fatal punch, my way of knocking that prick out.

I turn the box upside down, find my sharpest kitchen knife and slice along the tape at the bottom, and then gently, I open the underside of the box.

I pull out reams of paper to find a bottle of whisky. Ledaig, the brand Nathaniel posted about on Instagram.

So this *is* what he's been ordering. Seems he's doing quite a bit of drinking in homage to his father.

I hold the bottle, feeling its cool glass in my hands, the heft of it.

Then I find the things I need: my drill, some superglue, brown tape. A dozen prescription sleeping tablets, which I crush and dissolve into a few tablespoons of water.

And then I get to work.

I clamp the bottle upside down firmly between my legs and, using my drill, I make a small hole through its base. It takes two seconds – a high-pitched whizz, a skimming dust of glass – and it's done.

I place my drill down and blow the glass particles away, and then I feed the crushed sedatives through the hole.

Biting my lip for the tricky part, I plug the hole with superglue and watch it dry, tapping it here and there to make sure its smooth, fixed, solid. I do that again and again, making sure the hole is completely sealed and secure.

And then I breathe.

I turn the bottle the right way up. It looks normal and nothing leaks. I shake it a little, but the hole really is airtight. Perfect.

You can barely even see it, not that I expect Nathaniel would check the bottom of the bottle.

Smiling to myself, I place it back in the box, and cover it with the paper as before. I seal the package with a small amount of fresh brown tape, hoping Nathaniel won't notice anything's up.

And then, with a spring in my step, I head back out.

I have a delivery to make.

CHAPTER TWELVE

Nathaniel is his typical charming self as he signs for his package. All bright, fake smiles and even another 'thanks, dude,' as I leave.

Thanks, dude. I won't have to put up with that for much longer.

I feel a satisfaction like nothing I've experienced for a while as I drive away.

I flick through radio stations, trying to find something that fits my mood.

I bypass a few irritating pop songs. No offence to Swifties, but 'Shake It Off' really isn't my thing. I land on an old classic: 'You Sexy Thing' by Hot Chocolate. Modern pop can't compete with the likes of this.

I turn the volume up, getting into the music. Singing along and grooving in my van. A few other drivers look my way, smirk, but I couldn't care less. I feel good.

I had been planning to go straight home, but I'm too fired up. I want to do something.

And so I park up by Saint Leonards beach and on a whim, I get some fish and chips from a cheap nearby joint, with strip lighting, scratched chrome, a faded linoleum floor. But the cod and chips I order look delicious and fresh. Wrapped up, my meal's warm in my hands and the scent of vinegar makes my mouth water. I realise I'm famished. I need this.

When was the last time I ate anything other than Greggs? Anything other than beans on toast?

I sit on a bench on the promenade, adjust my coat against the chill, and devour my meal. Inhale it, as people say these days. The fish is crispy and delicious, each chip's perfect. It's been God knows how long since I enjoyed a meal so much.

Eventually, placing the empty wrapper beside me, I look out to sea. The moon is visible over the ocean, faint, but visible. It's large and full.

I hadn't realised it was a full moon tonight, but it would make sense.

What is it Serena Soulful always says about full moons? They're symbolic of renewal, growth, a heightened time for creativity, emotion, release. I guess she's right.

I sit for a while, trying to ignore the chill. The sky darkens and the sea rushes keenly over the beach, the tide coming in. Against the darkness, the moon begins to glow.

I didn't used to, but I've grown to quite like Hastings in winter.

Summer is all pomp and ironic hipsters posing at the amusement arcade and lounging on picnic blankets on the beach. It's displaced artists staying in Airbnbs, having a reprieve from London. It's tourists looking for a quirky weekend break or a cheap family holiday in a place they hope is up and coming.

But winter's different, it's harsher, quieter. The weather sorts the wheat from the chaff. The peripheral people fall away, and the true locals remain.

Without the gloss of sunshine and the vibrancy of the summer influx, the place gets colourless, rough. The arcades shut down, as does the crazy golf, most of the restaurants, even some of the big hotels. It's like a ghost town, and the druggies and drunks who've survived generations of poverty and disadvantage come out of the woodwork, reclaiming their streets. Only a few weeks ago, I saw a couple of smackheads shooting up on the beach in broad daylight, cawing seagulls circling overhead.

Without all the other stuff going on, the real Hastings shows itself. McDonald's starts heaving, one of the few places to eat that's open all year around, and the queue spilling from the Job Centre becomes harder to ignore.

By spring, pretty much everyone is gasping for the sun to come up, for the hipsters and artists and tourists to flood the town and distract everyone from the cold, harsh misery of the place.

But I like it. I like the rawness, the lack of pretence. The dark skies and dour, deserted beaches.

It's getting colder now, and my coat really isn't cutting it. I should go, but, shivering, I look out at the cargo ships, shadowy outlines in the distance, soon to be engulfed by the night. There are some teenagers, laughing further along the beach, sheltered by an underpass, drinking from a bottle of something they wouldn't want their parents to know about. A passing dog walker throws a ball for his whippet, who doesn't bother to chase it.

I feel strange, almost disconnected from myself. Here but not here, aware of everything, attuned to the fabric of life, its texture. The scene before me is beautiful in its own way. It's fragile, poetic.

Or perhaps I'm just projecting.

Because right now, as I sit here, belly full, philosophical, I have a feeling Nathaniel might be settling down to watch something on TV. A match, perhaps. He'll be drinking his whisky, getting sozzled, catatonic. And soon, everything will be different.

I could be wrong, of course. I'll be the first to admit that my plan has flaws.

Perhaps Nathaniel won't even open his bottle of Ledaig at all. Perhaps he'll stash it at the back of a cupboard for another time and completely forget about it.

Or perhaps he'll invite some friends over, some woman from the gym, and someone will call an ambulance the moment he loses consciousness.

Or, perhaps, things will go exactly as I expect they will, and my plan will work out fine.

Maybe it's the full moon or my positive, manifesting attitude, but I feel like I've got this. Tonight is my night.

The whippet starts barking at another dog, a yappy chihuahua, who shrieks in return, and I get up, dump my wrapper in a nearby bin, and head off.

I need to get home. Warm up, have a coffee, and prepare for the next stage of my plan.

CHAPTER THIRTEEN

For once, Serena Soulful annoys me.

Tonight's topic on *The Rising Sun Show* is karma. Serena believes that whatever you put out into the universe, you get back. That you'll have to pay a price for every bad deed, either in this life or the next, and I can't help finding her attitude irritating.

Karma has always felt like a lie weak people tell themselves. A comforting illusion peddled by losers who don't have the balls to fight back. Believing bad people might pay a price in the next life feels almost like Christianity. Heaven and hell bullshit.

I turn the podcast off. No one's perfect I guess, not even Serena Soulful. I listen to some music instead, killing time.

I have a few coffees and at around 1am, I slip out of my flat, as quietly as possible so I don't disturb my neighbours. I don't need anyone knowing I was out tonight.

The street is weirdly still and quiet. A cold mist clings to the windows of parked cars.

I wrap my scarf tighter around my neck, pulling down the ridiculous bucket hat I'm wearing, a relic of Bob's Bazaar. I never quite managed to get rid of all the shop's stock. Perhaps I just wasn't ready to let it go, and so for years I've had boxes of paraphernalia gathering dust in the corners of my flat. If you need two hundred beaded bracelets or fifty picnic blankets, I'm your man!

Hippy clothes used to be quite popular among my customers. You know the sort of thing: tent-like hareem trousers, patchwork tops, big hemp wool jumpers. Not exactly my style, but people seemed to like them. They enjoyed letting their inner hippy out for a trip to the sea.

I figured it would be good to dress completely out of character tonight, just in case any CCTV cameras pick up on me. The bucket hat and scarf do a pretty good job of making me look totally indecipherable, as do the dark, loose trousers.

I make my way to Samuel Close, nervous about what I'm going to find, and simultaneously trying not to be nervous at all.

Thoughts become reality, as Serena Soulful always says. *Confidence is key.*

And so, as I walk through the dark streets, I tell myself that everything is going to go exactly to plan. I've got this.

By the time I reach Samuel Close, I'm feeling pumped, positive, and pretty much unstoppable, actually. The street is pin-drop quiet. Lights off, curtains drawn.

It's a kind of trimmed hedge, lights out by 10pm, sort of neighbourhood.

It's not the type of area people like me usually frequent, and my heart starts to beat faster as I reach number 19.

Clearly tomorrow is bin day. Everyone's left their bins out, except Nathaniel.

Has he forgotten? Or was he simply too out of it? I have a feeling it's the latter. Nathaniel doesn't strike me as the kind of man who misses bin day.

The light in his front room is on too, the only light still glowing on the street.

Interesting.

Again, Nathaniel doesn't seem like he'd leave the light on in his front room. Either he's up late or he passed out. Just as planned.

Head down, I get closer.

My chest feels tight, almost overwhelmingly so, as I reach the front drive. I have a sudden vision of him bursting out of his house, storming across his manicured lawn, screaming at me. Ridiculous, but I'm panicking.

Breathe.

A deep breath, right into my belly. There are three chambers of the lungs: the superior, middle and inferior lobes. Just like Serena Soulful always says. I draw my breath right into the inferior lobe. Right into the depths of my stomach.

A few deep breaths of cool refreshing air is all it takes for me to calm down.

I push open the front gate and, looking over my shoulder to check none of the neighbours' curtains are twitching, I creep down the garden path and peer through the window.

Nathaniel is partially obscured by a net curtain, but I see him. He's *just* like I imagined.

He's passed out on the sofa, the whisky bottle and a glass on a coffee table. Along with a plate of food he's polished off.

I tap the window, but he doesn't stir. He doesn't move at all.

Perfect!

I turn and head back down the street.

I have to pick a lock to get into the house, but I may as well pick the one on the back door. The last thing I need is a neighbour calling the police.

Creeping back down the shadowy street, I make my way towards the field at the back of your house, where I retrieve a shovel from my bag and set about recreating my burrow.

I have to take off my hat to slip under the fence though, and I'm relieved when I get to the other side, safe in the darkness of your garden.

I creep to your back door and ready myself for the tricky bit. Well, not that tricky.

I've been into picking locks for a while, and not in a criminal way.

I learnt how to do it as a teenager. Nothing dodgy. Nothing like that.

It was just one of those weird skills I picked up from hours spent alone. Like knots. Want a clove hitch or a bowline? I'm your guy. I even decided to teach myself calligraphy at one point.

The lock-picking thing has come in handy on occasion, though. I once impressed an ex-girlfriend in London by getting her back in her flat this time she got locked out, using a few angled bits of wire and an old credit card. Or at least, she acted impressed at the time. When we eventually broke up, she used it as ammunition, evidence of my creepiness, telling me what a "weird burglar freak" I was. Her loss.

My lock-picking skills are a bit rusty these days, but good old Google sorted me out. There's a plethora of handy tips from wrong'uns online – criminals posing as helpful blokes giving advice to silly klutzes who keep losing their keys.

Personal safety really is just an illusion, a comforting lie we tell ourselves.

Mentally, I've practiced picking this lock dozens of times, but reality is a different story.

You have to believe to achieve. Serena Soulful's voice comes to me, almost like she's with me in spirit, like I'm channelling her.

I can do this, I remind myself, as I look over my shoulder, take the lock-picking tools from my pocket, and get to work.

Inserting my pick into the lock, I rattle it around, familiarizing myself with the pins. I start to sweat. The pins don't seem to be moving and I can't quite get a feel for the lock. But no, I keep going.

I just need to find that sweet spot. That moment when the pins click, dislodging, and I can turn my tension wrench and twist the lock open. It's not that hard. The most important thing is keeping your cool.

And yet, why won't the pins fucking move?

A shadow passes to my right. I hear a rustle.

My stomach drops, right through my fucking asshole, and my blood cools.

I turn, paralysed. I'm terrified, my eyes widen, when I see a fox. A fucking fox.

Its eyes glint.

We stare at each other for a second, and then it turns and bolts.

A fox.

A fucking fox.

My heart reanimates and starts beating again.

I focus on the lock. This fucking annoying lock.

Come on. Come on...

I rattle my pick, again and again, trying to stay calm. And then finally, just as I'm thinking I might have to go home, abandon this whole fucking thing, something clicks. The pins click, and I twist my tension wrench, not breathing as I turn it. I press down on the door handle, and the door opens.

I'm in! I've never been happier to see a pristine IKEA kitchen in my life.

The sound of the TV bleeds from next door. A football match, a droning commentator.

I creep forward, exhaling. Thank God, I'm in.

My heart thuds as I move towards the sitting room. I'm still a bit concerned about Nathaniel.

What if he's somehow roused and he's waiting for me, menacing, armed with a baseball bat?

But no. As I creep into the sitting room, peering around the door, I find him lying prostrate on the sofa, just as before.

The whisky bottle on the table is half-empty. He's had *a lot* of sleeping tablets by the looks of it.

I flick the light off and tiptoe towards the curtains, keeping my eyes on him.

He's still, incredibly still. Is he dead?

I draw the curtains and turn the TV off, shuddering. I've always hated the sound of football matches. The canned commentators, the gormless cheers. Weirdly, it makes me feel almost car sick, claustrophobic. It reminds me of my dad.

I get closer to Nathaniel. He's drooling, which makes me smirk. He looks so pathetic, a far cry from his pouting Instagram shots. He's pale and flaccid. Even his fake tan is straining to make him look particularly alive.

I crouch down and peer at his chest. He's breathing, softly. Weakly, by the looks of it.

I decide to get the next part over as quickly as possible.

I'm no fan of Nathaniel, that much is obvious, but I don't exactly want to kill him. I don't take pleasure in murder. It's not me.

I'm not a violent man, a sadist. And I mean, as far as murders go, what I'm about to do is incredibly gentle, merciful. A nice way to die. Nathaniel won't have a clue. One minute he was watching the footy, the next, gone. He'll have died doing exactly what he loved.

It's a kindness to kill him this way. A lot of people's deaths are much worse.

He does deserve a harsher end, but I don't need this getting complicated. I just need to get it done.

So, I take some heroin I scored a few weeks ago from those smackheads I saw shooting up on Saint Leonards beach. They were pretty friendly actually, although it was probably the high.

They took me to Warrior Square and the next thing I knew I was in a grubby basement flat scoring from a bedraggled man with a Bukowski quote tattooed across his chest: 'Find what you love and let it kill you'. Drugs, in his case? He reassured me over and over that 'this is the good stuff' as he bagged up enough smack to keep a pretty hardcore addict going for a week. More than enough to kill in one dose.

So that's what Nathaniel's getting. A big, generous helping of Saint Leonards' finest.

I get some water from the kitchen. Naturally, I'm wearing gloves. Don't want to be leaving prints around here. Then I sit in the armchair and carefully and quietly prepare the dose, burning it up on a teaspoon. I think about you, Natalie, as I do this. I think of you sitting here, in this spot. I have an image of you in pyjamas, a pink pair you've got on in one of your Facebook pictures. They hugged your curves beautifully, if you don't mind me saying. Your hair was plaited in a long messy braid, dangling over your shoulder. Your bedtime look.

You're so beautiful. You really have no idea, do you?

I can't wait to sit with you, like that, in pyjamas. Feel your body against mine. Our legs intertwined, perhaps? Watching something trashy on TV. I can't think of anything more lovely. I wonder what you smell like.

I hold the thought as I approach Nathaniel and sit down delicately beside him. He doesn't move a muscle.

One of his arms is splayed by his side, palm up. He's almost making this too easy for me, Natalie! Or maybe the universe has just conspired in our favour.

I spot the blueish hue of a vein in the pit of his elbow, slip the needle in, and plunge. Done.

I edge back a bit and watch, weirdly fascinated.

Nathaniel sputters and jerks. A full body spasm, like an electrocuted corpse. I hold my breath, terrified, and then he just goes limp. Completely limp. His breathing tails off. His skin whitens. And after a bit, his lips go blue. Ha!

It's strange, Natalie. Like watching the sky darken earlier. Everything just loses its colour and hue, dissipates. It has that poetic feel. That ennui.

I look at Nathaniel for longer than I should, but it's morbidly satisfying to see how white he goes.

And then I tidy up the loose ends. Add a bit of theatre.

A tourniquet around his arm (a bit of rope I got from the hardware store down the road).

I put a baggie of smack at the back of the coffee table drawer, and a few pills of speed, thrown in as an extra by my trusty friend. I need to make it look like Nathaniel's been falling off the wagon for a while.

I pour the rest of the whisky down the loo next door and flush. I don't need the police finding spiked liquor. I decide to take the bottle with me, just in case they test it somehow or spot the hole at the bottom. It might be nice to have a souvenir of tonight, anyway.

When the police do go over this scene, they'll find a sad ex-addict with a fucked-up life who fell off the wagon and tried to numb his pain, taking it all too far. Just another one of life's losers.

It almost slips by mind, but I flick the telly back on, just for added authenticity, and then, to the sound of football cheers, I leave.

CHAPTER FOURTEEN

I give you some time to grieve.

Nathaniel may have been a prick, but he was still your husband, your childhood sweetheart, the father of your child. Even though he screamed at you, beat you and made your life a living hell, it's still going to take a while for you to adjust.

I wish I could be there for you, Natalie. I really do.

Just know that you're all I think about. I check your Facebook profile first thing when I wake up and last thing at night, and hundreds of times in between.

I killed Nathaniel on Friday night, and you post about his death on Wednesday.

My heart is breaking as I write this. I can't believe I'm typing these words. On Sunday, Nathaniel was found dead at home... He was too young to die and as you can imagine, I'm devastated. I've lost my husband, my partner of ten years. Cara has lost her daddy. We're so heartbroken. I'll post some more soon, but just letting you guys know. I know this is hard for you to hear. Love you guys xxx

Heartbroken... Really?

I have to admit, Natalie, that stings a bit, although, I'm mostly just happy there's not a whisper of 'murder' in what you've written. Looks like it was all just a big, sad accident.

You post quite a lot of fairly nauseating stuff over the next few days. I'm not being rude, I get it. This is a difficult time for you. But it is a little hard to witness your sentimentality.

You share pictures of you and Nathaniel from happier days with captions like, *'still can't believe you're gone'.*

What's with the 'you'? As though you're speaking to Nathaniel's ghost? As though your profile is for his eyes only.

It's a bit odd, Natalie. But again, you are grieving. And grief is strange and unsettling, even when it comes to monsters like Nathaniel.

A week after your post about Nathaniel's death, you share a shot of your kitchen, full to the brim with bunches of flowers. It's beautiful. You've added a caption: *'It's like a florist in here. You guys are so kind. Love you all so much xxx'.*

Then, you post about the funeral.

A ceremony to be held at All Saints the following weekend. Nothing about what's happening to Nathaniel's remains. Direct cremation would have been a nice detail. Get that body reduced to ash ASAP, before any nosy coroners take a closer look. Not that I'm too worried. Even if, at any point, anyone did suspect anything, it's not like they'd point the finger at me. Me, of all people! You don't even know me.

In the week leading up to the funeral, you start posting links to songs that, apparently, are on Nathaniel's funeral playlist, and frankly, are way too good for the likes of him.

Live Forever, by Oasis. *Hallelujah*, by Jeff Buckley. *Wish You Were Here*, by Pink Floyd. *Where Is My Mind?* by The Pixies.

I mean, really? The Pixies? Nathaniel does not strike me as the type, Natalie. He seems more, I don't know... Radio One. Chase & Status. Rudimental. Lewis Capaldi.

I start getting worried that Nathaniel's death has turned him into some kind of martyr in your eyes. What if it's had a cleansing effect? Absolved him of his sins?

What if the whole thing's backfired? What if you think he felt so bad about the way he treated you and Cara that he topped himself? What if you start pining for him? Forget about his failings. Truly miss him.

Fuck.

I slack off work for a bit. Stop accepting shifts.

I've been plugging away at this stupid job day in, day out, for years. It's about time I had a break.

I drive by Samuel Close a few times. I'm not stupid, I'm hardly going to hang about, sit at the end of the road like before. But I pass your house now and then, hoping I might get lucky and catch a glimpse of you.

Eventually, I do.

You're standing in your front garden, talking to a neighbour and Natalie! You look resplendent. You're smiling, laughing, as though you don't have a care in the world. No one would know your husband just died. You're radiant. Ten years younger. Reborn.

An angel in leggings and a hoodie, your hair bundled into a bun.

Wow...

I smile to myself as I drive away. A big, wide, goofy smile, knowing I've done the right thing.

A few days later, I notice that the mood has started turning on your Facebook page.

Someone tags you in a tribute, some saccharine post featuring a shot of a dove and a lament to a 'pure soul'. To my utter, utter joy, you reply, '*he was no saint*', and soon after remove the tag completely.

Oh, Natalie. My Natalie.

You go a bit quiet after that, frustratingly so.

The funeral comes and goes, relatively undocumented. Selfies at a funeral is mercifully not a trend yet, and aside from a bunch of '*thinking of you*' posts that appear on your page, no one would really know the funeral was happening.

I'm half-tempted to drive down, sit outside the church, have a little spy, but it's too risky. Too stupid.

Instead, I spend the day meditating, re-reading *The Upanishads*, and chill out with a bit of yoga in the evening – bliss.

Maybe the funeral gave you all the closure you need, because you stop even mentioning Nathaniel afterwards. Your Facebook page is all about Cara.

Pictures of Cara painting at the kitchen table, at the park, dressing up in your dresses, swaddled in them. It's adorable. Cara looks healthier too, happier. Just like you do. It makes me feel all kinds of warm and fuzzy inside, Natalie, I can't even tell you.

I start wondering if I should make a move. Introduce myself into your life in a more traditional manner? I need to do it soon. If I don't, someone else will spot their chance and swoop in, and I can't have that. Not after everything I've done for you.

I can't quite figure out how to go about it, though.

I write '*help me figure out how to meet Natalie*' on a piece of paper, fold it up, and put it in my manifestation pot, knowing an answer will come to me.

And then, something happens that completely snaps me out of thoughts of you.

I get a call from my old landlord. Nigel from Bob's Bazaar. The estate agent next door is downsizing and no longer needs my old shop as office space. So, Nigel's looking to rent it out again. And for old time's sake, he thought he'd see if I was interested.

His voice goes all mushy and low and he explains that he always felt bad about 'selling out'. That he'd love to see my 'quirky, funny little shop open again' and would do me a good rate, 'a favour for an old pal'. I think he always did feel a bit guilty at having turfed me out.

It's hard to describe how that conversation felt, Natalie. I cried. My throat seized up and tears started pouring.

It took me completely by surprise.

I'm pretty zen these days, often to the point of numbness. I feel dead inside a lot of the time. The only thing that really moves me is you.

But the thought of having my shop back is invigorating. I imagine fairy lights twinkling, the smell of incense burning. Sitting behind the counter, feeling real, feeling human. The ding of the door. Chit-chat with customers. Going for walks along the beach at the end of the day.

I didn't realise quite how much I'd missed it until tears soaked my cheeks.

I tried to hide my emotion, but Nigel picked up on the tremor in my voice, and then he got emotional too. Slashed the rate to something ridiculous, clearly getting soft in his old age. And so I agreed, because, why not?

I miss my shop and it's time for a change. I have enough cash stashed away to get me started, to buy stock. Quite a lot of cash, actually. Half the time I've worked just for the sake of it. To not go mad at home. Telling myself I'm saving up for a proverbial rainy day.

'What have you been doing with yourself, anyway?' Nigel asks, once we both calm down.

'Don't see you around The Albion much anymore.'

He's right, I've kept myself to myself the past few years. I used to be an Albion regular and then at some point, I stopped going.

'Oh, just been busy, you know. Doing a bit of this, a bit of that.'

I find myself not wanting to talk about being a courier, not at all. I find myself wanting to forget all about it.

A silence passes and I can feel Nigel's awkwardness. Will he pry? Will he probe? But, no, he leaves it. He probably assumes I've been up to no good. Maybe he doesn't want to know.

'Alright, mate!' He laughs. 'So, want to go for a pint? Do the paperwork?'

I smile, grinning down the phone.

And, well, I guess... I guess I'm back in the game.

CHAPTER FIFTEEN

Over a few pints of Guinness, I sign the lease. And then, on the way home, I delete the delivery app.

Just like that. Gone. Uninstalled.

My last payment has already come through so it's not like they even need my bank details.

So, I delete everything. And that whole chapter of my life is over. Lost in the ether, like it never happened at all.

It's laughable, and yet I don't laugh. In fact, my stomach squirms.

Why did I ever tolerate such meaninglessness?

When I get home, my black beanie hat and sunglasses that I keep by the front door for work catch my eye and I find them revolting. Utterly revolting. Offensive.

I pick up the glasses, and in a moment that feels not quite real, a little performative, and yet satisfying nonetheless, I snap them, clean in two, right across the bridge. And then, because I can, I break the arms off. And snap each of them in two as well. And then I laugh. A bitter, wild laugh, and I pop the bits of sunglasses into my hat and toss the whole lot in the bin.

Over. Done. Just like that.

In the following days, I get in touch with my old stockists and start placing orders. Boxes of crystals, sticks of rock, dreamcatchers, postcards, all the usual stuff. I buy fairy lights, garlands of plastic ivy, little mirrors in the shapes of stars and moons. Even fake flowers. Nicer stuff than I had before, girlier. I want to make the shop pretty, more Gwyneth Paltrow and less Uri Gellar. I want you to like it, Natalie.

I go to a stockist in Brighton and get box upon box of seaside tat, haggling the vendor down.

It helps that I have my van. I deposit boxes at the shop, as well as the old stock that's been cluttering my flat for years. Maybe I kept it for a reason, for this moment.

The shop isn't what it used to be. It's a bit run down, but I can restore it to its former glory with a bit of DIY. I just need to give the walls a lick of paint, put in a new carpet.

All I think about is the shop, I can't stop thinking about it. It's like my heart's been reanimated, reinvigorated, and some dark cloud that I didn't even fully realise was hanging over me has lifted.

I get so swept up in preparing for the re-opening that I forget to go on your Facebook page. Not completely. I still look at it a few times a day, but not like before. It's not that I've forgotten about you, Natalie. Of course not. You're part of my fantasies.

As I inspect boxes of snow globes and crystals, I imagine you popping into the shop, browsing, having a chat, kissing me over the counter. I imagine a life for us, in which we're both happier, fulfilled. You, getting out and about again. Me, with my business.

It's almost like Nathaniel's death has set us both free. It's like some horrible curse has been lifted.

After a long day, I pour myself a large glass of Pinot Noir. A good brand this time, from a nice new off-licence, not even Tesco. What can I say? There's something exciting in the air now. Something that makes me feel like splashing out.

But funnily enough, I probably need something strong for what I'm about to read.

Natalie, Natalie, Natalie...

Your latest Facebook post is pretty hard to swallow.

Some days I wake up and feel like I can do this, I feel like I've got this. I'm determined to be strong and smile for Cara. But then there are other days when everything is too much and I can't believe he's gone. It feels like I've lost my rock and I feel so, so alone.

What the fuck, Natalie?

Your rock? Your ROCK?

He beat you. He beat you! He screamed at you like you were trash.

I pace around the room. Seething, fucking seething.

Your rock! Your fucking rock.

When I finally calm down, which involves loudly cursing and a few guttural groans that no doubt alarm my neighbours, I refill my glass and sit back down at my laptop.

Bracing myself, I take in the comments.

Erica Cooper: *Hang on in there, babe. Thinking of you.*

Chris Brook: *Be strong, Nat. I know it's not easy, but you can do this. Time does heal. Trust me Xx*

Anita Singh: *Nat, you poor thing. My heart goes out to you xx*

And then one. One that makes all this pain somehow worthwhile.

From your mum. I've seen her tagged in your pictures before. She looks good for her age, which bodes well.

Emma Knowles: *Oh honey... Let's just hope the Saint Leonards Bereavement Group helps on Thursday. You've got this, sweetheart.*

You've replied.

Natalie Sutherland: *I really hope it'll help. Thanks mum. xx*

So...

You're going to a grief support group. And I'm beaming, grinning, wine-stained teeth on full display.

Because yet again, Natalie, as it always does with me and you, the darkness has given way to light, to sunrise.

I've seen my way in. My manifestation pot has delivered.

I'm joining the support group.

It's time for my mum to 'die'.

CHAPTER SIXTEEN

My mum's been dead to me a long time. God knows what she's doing with herself these days. She might genuinely be dead for all I know, although it would have probably got back to me somehow.

But either way, it's time to kill her off.

Nothing too dramatic. Just something sad, sudden. Tragic, yet mundane.

After a bit of Google research, I decide on rapidly advancing lung cancer.

Just appeared, out of nowhere, bless her. Spread to her liver, her brain, bones. Lit up her body like a Christmas tree. Within a few months, she was dead.

I don't mean to sound cynical, but I bet that'll get a tear out of you, Natalie. Out of everyone.

I read stories of people who've lost their loved ones to cancer, pinch bits of their heartbreak. Little details. Raw descriptions of physical degeneration, emotional punchlines.

Then, I tell my story to my bathroom mirror. A gut-wrenching, troubled, choked monologue. My eyes fill up.

I could have been an actor, Natalie. I really could have. I could see myself on stage at The Old Vic.

I decide to do a few dress rehearsals, I guess you could call them, down the pub. Break the news to Nigel and a couple of others.

My performance must have been Oscar level because I lost track of the number of drinks I had bought for me. The number of pats on the back, the condolences. It was surprisingly nice.

It's not like I got any sympathy when I cut my mother off, I didn't even tell anyone. I have my reasons for breaking contact, no one who severs contact with their parents doesn't. But no one wants to grieve with you when you're grieving for a parent who's still alive. In fact, no one wants to hear about it at all. Estrangement is a grubby, thorny subject. The loneliest form of grief.

But now that everyone thinks my mum's officially dead, I allow myself to talk about her for the first time in years.

And I admit to her flaws.

'She had a temper,' I tell an old friend in a hushed corner of The Albion when I'm on my third or fourth pint. An understatement, really.

But after another drink, I find myself opening up about some of the beatings, the neglect, and my mate cares. He really cares, he commiserates. I see real compassion in his eyes. They're soft, glossy with it.

He tells me about his father, a violent man. Inflicted lashings with a belt until he bled. In the end, we both cry a little. We open up in a way we've never done before. I don't tell him everything, but I tell him enough. And weirdly, I feel less alone. Significantly less alone.

I never knew grieving could be so good. I should probably kill off my father sometime soon, too.

CHAPTER SEVENTEEN

I call the support group the next day and ask if I can join.

A woman answers, Sandra Jones. She sounds a little rushed, terse, and she tells me the group on Thursday is full, but they have a new one starting in a few weeks, which I might like to join instead. This is *not* okay.

So I put on the waterworks. My breathing gets shaky. And to be honest, real panic and genuine pain has set in.

I tell her I don't think I'll be able to cope. I can't wait that long.

'Please, I'm just... I'm really, really struggling,' I sob.

'Okay, of course.' She softens. 'We're meeting at 4pm on Thursday here at the community centre. You're welcome to come along.'

And just like that, I'm in.

CHAPTER EIGHTEEN

It's strange, trying to figure out what to wear. Trying to look at once attractive and pained.

Obviously, I can't exactly wear a traditional date get-up to the support group: best trousers, a nice shirt, decent blazer. No, I need to look like I'm falling apart.

It helps that I've been run off my feet, trying to get everything ready for the shop. All the DIY, driving around, picking up stock. It's been surprisingly exhausting, and it's left me with some handy little eye bags and a general air of weariness that would probably be a hindrance to any kind of regular romantic introduction.

All the shop stuff's got me leaner, too. I feel fitter, healthier. My depression has lifted, and I've found I'm not eating as much or as badly. I'm driving past Greggs without stopping in. I was pretty much carb and caffeine-fuelled as a courier, but not anymore. I've caught my reflection a few times in the shop window and been pleasantly surprised. I almost look like the old me.

I decide to wear my best jeans. A nice-fitting pair of vintage Levi's, with a baggy jumper. It's worn and bobbling and a little grungy, but also a turquoise shade that's an exact match for my eyes and I know looks good. It's one of the reasons I've kept the jumper at all, despite the fact it's long past its best.

I haven't showered and my hair's ever so slightly greasy. I ruffle it, mussing it up as I inspect my reflection, making myself look even more unkempt, with a touch of hairspray and artfulness, of course.

Considering the shabbiness of my look, I really don't look at all bad.

I have a certain charm, I'm aware of that. The number of women I've bedded would testify to it.

When I put myself out there, I tend to attract attention. But I'm an acquired taste. I'm a bit Jarvis Cocker. Scruffy hair, pouty, effete. I'm the kind of man who's incredibly sexy to the sort of woman who likes Tim Burton films and appreciates the music of Patti Smith, Nick Cave, The Smiths. I appeal to women who wear thrifted clothes and possibly have a nose ring. I have a certain vibe, and my look's got me laid far more than my personality ever could. I wonder what you'll make of it, though, Natalie. I'm a far cry from the nouveau riche, Love Island charm of Nathaniel. But perhaps you fancy a change.

I may be fifty but for romantic purposes, I generally tend to identify as forty-four. No one ever questions it. It's quite remarkable how ageless a life of childless solitude can be. Even with my penchant for Guinness and Pinot Noir.

Most of the women I've dated have been passing FILTH. Down for the summer, unable to hack winter. Or me.

The last was Sarah. Quite a while back now, back when I had the shop. I knew she was FILTH the moment I saw her. Sitting on a bench on the pier, a lost look in her eyes. She had that FILTH look. Dressed for the beach – floral smock, Birkenstocks, red lipstick, big shades. Locals don't really dress like that.

I sat down next to her, struck up a conversation. It turned out she'd been made redundant from her marketing job, had a boss who'd bullied her. She was down on her luck, traumatised by corporate London. Wasn't particularly close to her parents, didn't have anywhere to turn. She felt some time by the sea would be good, healing. Thought maybe she'd move here, do something different.

Naturally, I could relate. I told her about my own experience, gave her the empathy and understanding she so desperately needed.

We had a fun summer, very larky. All sunbathing, splashing in the sea, walks on Camber Sands, picnics, pints, gigs.

And then winter came and the cracks started to show and eventually, she moved back to London. She fell for me, loved me apparently, but I had to tell her I didn't feel that way. I didn't feel she was my soulmate.

She laughed at that.

'There's no such thing as a soulmate for you, Bob,' she insisted, sitting in her Airbnb, her stuff mostly in bags, matter of fact to the point of bored. 'You don't have a soul.'

I step outside. It's a cold night, which will add to my general worn look, and as I get in my van, I try to get some tears flowing. I scroll through my memory for something tragic. My whole life is a bit of a tragedy really, but nothing much resonates anymore. Most of my pain's been blunted over the years. But then I think of Rex. Rex. How did I forget? My lovely old dog. He was pretty much the only source of love I had growing up and, well, he got run over when I was eleven, because my dad 'forgot' to close the gate one afternoon. To be honest, I think he just got sick of Rex's barking.

Anger starts pulsing through me, and I realise my mouth's gone tight, and my chest is rising and falling markedly. But I need tears. Actual tears, not anger.

I try not to think of my father. Focus on Rex, the softness of his fur. The wheaty smell of his belly after he'd been sleeping. His big, kind eyes, the colour of cellos. The face licks he used to give me. I loved everything about him, and he loved me. He really loved me. Such a pure love. Giving. Selfless.

My eyes prick with tears as I think about him. About what it would be like to see him again. Some afterlife reunion, him jumping into my arms.

My thoughts move me, and by the time I arrive at the community centre, I'm wiping tears from my eyes with the sleeve of my jumper.

I wonder if you're nearby, Natalie. Maybe looking out of the window. Do you see me? This weepy, attractive stranger, wandering in.

I head inside, trying not to think too much about you, or my nerves. I need to keep this about grief.

There are about ten chairs in a circle in the centre of the hall. Nothing but chairs, monkey bars against a wall, a fire exit, and a smell of rubber and bleach that takes me back to sports lessons at school. I don't see you, which strikes panic into my heart.

Where are you? I cannot have done all this crying for nothing.

Scanning the limp, hunched figures, double-checking, I'm considering doing a U-turn when a woman clocks me, her face lighting up with a big, welcoming smile. I can tell instantly that it's Sandra.

My face grimaces into a smile.

She comes towards me, waddling in too-tight polyester trousers, one of those long, flowy cardigans wafting with each step. She's wearing a lanyard.

'Bob?' she asks.

'Yes,' I croak, wanting to leave.

'I'm Sandra. It's good to meet you,' she says softly, patiently, as though speaking to a dumb child.

I stare at her, panicking, my stomach twisting. I can't do a full hour of fake grief. Not without Natalie.

'I know this is hard,' Sandra coos, touching my arm. 'Believe me, I know. But this is a safe space. Everyone's in the same boat.'

A safe space.

I already hate it here.

Sandra's soft, sympathetic eyes bore into me.

'Thank you,' I croak.

And then, Sandra's gaze shifts. She clocks someone over my shoulder, and her face lights up again. That full-beam compassion look.

'You must be Natalie?'

I turn, and there you are.

Chapter Nineteen

You barely look at me. You're focused on Sandra.

You seem nervous, out of breath, a bit panicked. You apologize a few times for being late.

Sandra tells you not to worry.

You're not wearing make-up and your eyes are puffy. Your hair's messy, like mine. It's greasy, bundled on the top of your head.

There's a smudge of moisturiser on your cheek that you haven't rubbed in. You must have got ready late, left in a hurry. You seem chaotic. You're in leggings, a shirt that looks like something you'd wear to an office, a big scarf, chipped nail polish. Nothing matches, it's all a bit rough around the edges. And yet, it's you.

You're here, in the flesh.

You may be tired and flustered, but if you knew how different you look to the first time I saw you, when you stood down the hall, barely there, ghostlike, then maybe you'd take some comfort in your progress. You've come a long way, Natalie. You really have.

We take our seats in the circle. Pretty much opposite each other.

I'm excited, Natalie, by your proximity. I'm worried I'm blushing, so I keep my head down. I keep thinking of that smudge of moisturiser on your face. How much I'd like to rub it in, cup your cheek, kiss you. But the thought is not appropriate.

Ridiculously, my cock stiffens. I cross my legs, bend forward, adjust my jumper over my groin, grateful I chose such a baggy one. For fuck's sake. You really do something to me, Natalie. Who gets an erection at a grief support group?

Sandra is saying something about the importance of sharing and support, and blah blah blah, but all I can think about is how much I'd like to have you against the monkey bars.

No. No. Think of Rex. Think of Rex...

I nod sagely to everything Sandra says, even though none of it, absolutely none of it, is going in.

'How are you doing today, Bob?' Sandra turns her attention to me. 'What brings you here?' Her voice is gentle, her face plastered with sympathy.

She clearly thinks I'm desperate to share after my pained phone call the other day.

I clear my throat. Keeping my legs crossed, I give an overview of my situation. My mother's sad demise, how it's affected me. How we didn't always have the best relationship, but her death has got to me nonetheless.

My routine is pretty well-rehearsed from the pub and my voice cracks in all the right places, but it's kind of true, actually. Memories of my mum have been coming up lately, ever since her 'death'. It has been a strange time. And of course, the best lies are always a blend of truth and fiction.

As I'm saying something about my childhood, back in Slough, I steal a glance at you, Natalie.

Your eyes are wide, your head tilted, and you're drinking in what I'm saying, as though every word resonates, and I have to struggle, really struggle, not to smile, not to beam with pride.

I look down at the scratched floorboards and focus on my story, but I've lost my thread. I mutter something about 'everything being so overwhelming, so hard' and trail off, adding a lip tremble.

Sandra thanks me for sharing and says something about grief being a 'journey'. She compliments me on my strength, my courage.

I nod forlornly and thank her, my voice a little choked, not from emotion, but more from the effort of suppressing a guffaw at how ridiculous this whole thing is.

I just want to hold you, Natalie. Tell you how wonderful you are.

We move through the group. There's Marg, a sweet old lady who looks like an extra on EastEnders. Lost her husband of fifty years recently to a stroke.

Fifi, whose son died while swimming in the sea – off his tits by the sound of it – at a beach party in Ko Pan Yang. She's devastated and in a bit of a state, slurring a little. It's pretty clear she's taken something. Some kind of downer, I'd imagine.

She tells the group she's been talking to pictures of her son. Sending text messages to his old number. Wearing his hoodies around the house.

None of it sounds healthy and it's a bit uncomfortable to hear. But Sandra seems to think Fifi's bizarre behaviour is a good thing, a sign she's 'facing her pain'.

There's Aleysha, who's struggling after the death of her dog, a hideous-sounding pug sausage dog cross. Her 'best friend', her 'angel', her 'baby'. She sobs, really sobs, and, funnily enough, I find myself crying with her as I think of Rex.

A couple of others share, too. Suzy, very depressed and grieving her sister, who died in a car crash. Adrian, whose wife passed a couple of months ago following a battle with Parkinson's. Ahmed, grieving his mother. Etcetera.

I glance at you and you're looking. You're looking right at me. Closely, as though assessing me in some way. I can't quite read your gaze.

Everyone's outpourings go over my head as I try to figure out what you think of me. You don't recognise me, do you? You haven't clocked me as your courier?

No. I look completely different now, without my shades, my beanie, my air of anonymity. There's no way you'd recognise me.

And then, it's your turn.

'Hi, I'm Natalie,' you say, with a sad, almost apologetic smile.

You look down at your lap. You've taken off your scarf and I notice you're wearing a locket. What does it contain? Please not pictures of Nathaniel.

'My husband... My husband passed away recently. He, umm...' You trail off, plucking at a loose thread on your leggings.

Sandra catches your eye and nods encouragingly.

'He overdosed.'

I smile ever so slightly. Everyone's eyes are on you. And yours are on your lap.

'He had issues with drugs back when he was younger. Didn't touch them for years, until recently. It was the anniversary of his dad's death. It hit him hard, and, well...'

You sound different in person. Maybe it's the grief, or maybe you just have a Facebook voice, but you sound softer, huskier.

'I'm trying to be strong. For Cara, my daughter,' you continue. 'But I don't know. Everything feels so... different. I keep expecting Nathaniel to burst through the door or call me. I don't like being alone. I find it so weird sleeping in our bed at night, all on my own. I haven't really been sleeping. I feel tired all the time.' You sigh.

'It gets easier,' Marg reassures you, with a sad smile.

'Yeah, I guess. My daughter's been intense. Luckily, my mum helps out. But it's not the same. It's just weird doing everything myself. Like, the washing machine stopped working the other day, and I didn't know how to fix it. I just broke down. I thought, "Nathaniel would have taken care of that" and it all just hit me.'

You flick a tear from your eye. My heart breaks for you, a little. But it doesn't sound like you're missing a husband, Natalie. It sounds like you need a handyman. Or, better, me.

Sandra says something about the importance of community and reaching out. Then Marg chimes in again with an admittedly quite sweet anecdote about how she couldn't get her lawnmower to work after her husband, John, died and so went over to the neighbour, who she'd never really spoken to, and asked for help. It turned out her neighbour was a widow too and now they're the best of pals. Even go to a knitting class together.

The story lightens the mood. You smile.

'I chat to my neighbour more now too,' you say. 'And my friends.'

Pepping up, you venture, 'You know, sometimes I have these moments, when I'm having a normal conversation and I'm laughing about something, and I realise I'm *not* thinking about Nathaniel. I'm not crying or sad, and then I feel terrible because I feel like I should be grieving *more.*'

You laugh, embarrassed.

Everyone starts chipping in. They know *exactly* what you mean. They get it. They've felt the same. You've opened some kind of dam with your words, Natalie, because now everyone's talking.

There's something special about you. You're magnetic. You have this energy I didn't even realise was there. Every hair on my body stands on end as I watch you, nodding, smiling, clicking with the group. I drink in your vibrancy.

'What about you, Bob?' Marg asks.

I turn to her, perplexed. Her eyes are creased, damp, mascara-smudged. What about me?

It takes me a second to realise I'm expected to contribute my own little anecdote to this guilt-at-not-grieving thing, too.

Shit.

'Yes...' I state, idiotically, trying to think of something to say.

And then it hits me.

'I'm reopening my shop. It's a sort of touristy shop. You know... Postcards, sticks of rock, buckets and spades, that kind of thing. I've been so swept up in decorating that sometimes I completely forget what I'm going through. I had the radio on the other day and I caught myself singing along to Doja Cat, and then I felt *awful.*'

It's kind of true. I did sing along to Doja Cat. Didn't feel awful though.

You laugh. A little snort laugh.

I look at you and our eyes lock. Something passes between us, a spark.

'What's Doja Cat?' Marg asks, and you laugh again.

CHAPTER TWENTY

The next week passes in a blur. I set up the shop in a happy daze, stringing up fairy lights and stocking the shelves. There's a spring in my step, and I catch myself smiling as I walk to the shop each morning, feeling a lightness I haven't felt for months. I even start frequenting a coffee shop down the road, run by a FILTH couple. I get matcha lattes, make chit-chat. The couple seem to warm to me, so much that they even throw in a free flapjack with my order every now and then. I'm a new man, Natalie. It's the you effect.

You're all I think about. I replay every second of the support group meeting in my mind. Every word, every look.

Being in your company was like crack. I didn't want it to end.

I wanted to say something to you at the end of the meeting, but Sandra cornered me. Started telling me how lovely it was to meet me, how good it was that I came along, how she hopes I found it helpful, etcetera. I think she might like me. Maybe I'm her type. Or perhaps, I delivered my dead mother story with such aplomb that she genuinely feels sorry for me.

As Sandra droned on about finding light in the darkness or some such shit, I noticed you duck out, waving sweetly at Marg and Aleysha as you left. My heart sank. But then I thought about it on the drive home and I realised I was grateful to Sandra. She saved me from myself. If it wasn't for her, I'd probably have run up to you like an excitable puppy, jumped the gun, looked too keen.

I think about that look we shared, the one that lasted a beat too long. I think of you laughing at my anecdote about the shop and I wonder if you've been thinking about me. That unusual man with his long fingers, turquoise eyes and messy, floppy hair. So different to Nathaniel. So new.

I know if it wasn't for the fact that I need to sort out the shop, I'd probably just sit around, daydreaming about you. Lighting candles. Writing poems. Manifesting.

But I need to get the shop ready: rip out the threadbare carpet, set up the counter, give the walls a lick of paint.

I need to sell my van too. If you and I are going to get close, then I have to get rid of it. I need to cut all ties between me and my old life.

I've put an ad up online. Hopefully someone will bite.

CHAPTER TWENTY-ONE

Thursday can't roll around quick enough.

I'll be honest, I'm not really in the mood for another grief-fest, but you left a comment on Facebook the other day, saying how the sessions are 'helping'. So I figure you'll be there again and if you're there, I'm there.

I decide to stay quiet this time, withdrawn. I don't have the energy for elaborate lies. Hopefully people will attribute my silence to my pain or something.

I take the bus this time since I've managed to get rid of my van. Sold it for a decent price to this couple from Eastbourne who want to convert it and do van life. Each to their own. I've got my eye on a decent-looking second-hand Renault, but I haven't locked the sale down yet.

Thanks to my out-of-practice approach to public transport, I end up arriving early. Which is good in a way. Hopefully you might too, and we can sit next to each other. But then people filter in, and the meeting kicks off without you and I'm worried I'm going to have to lie my way through a grief support group session for nothing. For absolutely nothing.

Marg, who's wearing far too much perfume today, starts droning on about how it slipped her mind that John wasn't here anymore, and she automatically bought his favourite steak and kidney pie from the shop the other day and then went home and cried about it. I wrack my brains for a decent reason to leave.

Aleysha starts telling us, yet again, how much she misses her dog. She's sobbing and I still haven't come up with a reason to get out of here, and then you show up, and my heart leaps. Soars.

You come in, heels clacking against the floorboards. You're wearing ankle boots, tight jeans. You've dressed up. You're flustered, apologetic, but you've dressed up. Maybe you've finally fixed your washing machine, but it looks like you've made an effort. You're still suitably lowkey, in jeans and a flattering cream jumper, but your outfit hugs your figure, and you must know that. You still have that locket on though, that stupid locket.

Your hair isn't greasy today, either. In fact, it's freshly washed, glossy, maybe even cut. It falls in pretty waves over your shoulders. You're wearing make-up too. Just a little, nothing obvious. A bit of blusher and mascara, some lipstick. You look beautiful.

It would be solipsistic of me to assume your efforts are for my benefit, and yet I'm hopeful they are.

You sit down, and I catch you looking my way. You quickly divert your gaze.

I smile to myself. I think you're into me!

I thought I might have been too old for you. Too weird. Too different. But it seems I've got your attention after all. Intrigued you...

Honestly, I thought I'd have to break you down more. Win you over with my sensitivity, my grief, my charm. But no, it seems you're interested already. I hope you're not considering me as a rebound, Natalie. I mean, that would be nice and all, and certainly hard to resist, but I want us to be more than that.

Marg dominates the conversation. She has a lot to say, and you and I are both happy to take a backseat.

But after a while, I feel I should probably contribute something. I proffer a titbit I saw on Reddit. Some woman wrote a letter to her dead dad containing all the things she wished she'd been able to say. I co-opt her experience, telling the group I did the same. That I cried a lot afterwards.

'Oh Bob, bless you,' Marg says, welling up.

She starts talking about John again. Says she wanted to send him a postcard when she went on holiday to Pembrokeshire over the summer, saying 'wish you were here'.

I glance at you. You smile sadly, sympathetically, but your eyes are dry.

You look so normal, Natalie. Have you really pulled yourself together? You look serene, subdued, *Mona Lisa* in a sea of Picassos.

Sandra turns to you. 'And Natalie, how have you been getting on?'

You say you're feeling better.

That you've been having 'darker' thoughts about Nathaniel.

I have to stop my eyes from widening. Darker? Really?!

You admit that your relationship 'wasn't perfect'. You say your grief had a bit of a 'halo effect' for a while. That it's complicated.

I want to cross the circle and fucking kiss you.

You tell the group you're getting better at being alone. That you fixed the washing machine.

You start talking about how Nathaniel liked you to stay home, take care of the house, but you've been thinking of going back to work. You trained as a nurse. You miss it. You mention that you've enrolled Cara into the local primary school and that she's really excited about meeting other kids. You explain that Nathaniel made you home school her before.

You're so positive and optimistic that it almost seems to unnerve the group. There's a silence. As though you've broken the script. I sit with my legs crossed and my arms folded. My hand is cupping my chin, covering my smile.

'That's... that's fantastic,' Sandra eventually says. 'How wonderful that you're feeling so strong, Natalie. Getting back into nursing sounds brilliant. I'm sure it would be great to have that to focus on.'

You nod beatifically. 'Exactly.'

I chime in.

'I've been finding working on my shop has really helped me. It's a good distraction.'

Sandra smiles. 'Oh yes. How's that coming along, Bob?'

I tell the group about painting the walls, ordering stock, etcetera. And then I have a brainwave.

I'm going to have a party.

'I'm opening doors next week, having a little opening party, canapes, prosecco, that kind of thing, if anyone wants to come along?'

By anyone, I mean you and only you.

'Obviously, we're all going through a hard time, but it would be nice. It'll just be low-key, a bit of fun. A small gathering, next Friday night.'

'I'd love to come!' Marg declares, her face lighting up.

'That's a lovely idea, Bob! Count me in,' Sandra enthuses.

'Sure, sounds cool. It's in Old Town, right?' Aleysha asks.

'Yeah, George Street.'

Fifi's up for it. And so are a few others whose names I can't even remember.

But what about you, Natalie? I glance your way, trying not to look pleading. *Please agree*, the last thing I need is to keep coming to these sessions every week.

'Sounds cool! I'll be there,' you say.

'Great,' I reply, keeping my tone casual. 'Next Friday, 7pm. Bob's Bazaar.'

Marg makes a note on her phone.

So does Aleysha.

And you. Well, you just look at me.

CHAPTER TWENTY-TWO

I've painted the walls a muted grey shade. Elephant's Breath actually, from Farrow & Ball. Had a nice new carpet fitted too, and the whole shop is twinkling with fairy lights.

The prettiest wares – dreamcatchers, crystals, candles, and soaps, are on full display. I can get out the tourist tat later.

Nigel and I prepare a buffet of Marks & Spencer's finest finger food. Not even Tesco. Only the best for Bob's Bazaar.

We put on some music, ambient, background stuff, and crack open one of the many bottles of prosecco we've lined up on a drinks table.

Of course, it's not just the grief support group coming, that would hardly be a party. The guys from the pub are coming along, too. I invited the FILTH couple from the café down the road. Nigel's been spreading the word along George

Street and a bunch of other business owners are stopping by. They all seem keen to support the latest enterprise.

'You've really come out of your shell, Bob,' Nigel comments, as he takes a sip of prosecco and adjusts a plate of sausage rolls.

I shrug, modest about the new leaf I've overturned.

'You were a bit of a moody bastard before.' He smirks. 'If you don't mind me saying.'

I hold up my hands in mock surrender. 'Guilty as charged!'

People soon start trickling in. Half of them I don't even recognise, but there are a few familiar faces. Shop owners who've been here for years.

I hand them glasses of prosecco and attempt to 'catch up'.

But all the while, I'm thinking about you. Where are you?

Eventually, the grief group starts to arrive. Marg first, then Sandra. Then Aleysha and Fifi.

But where are you?

I excuse myself from a conversation with the greengrocer from down the road and head over to the buffet table where I comfort eat a sausage roll. What if you don't come? What if you were just being polite when you said you'd be here? I shovel in another one. What if I've gone to all this effort for nothing? No. Please no.

I start demolishing yet another sausage roll, when the door dings. I look over and there you are.

This isn't exactly a Christmas party, but it is December, and you look like a Christmas fairy. You're adorable, Natalie. Absolutely adorable!

Your hair's all wavy, adorned with star-shaped clips, and you're wearing a cute red cardigan with the *tiniest* green miniskirt, spotted tights and sky-high stilettos. You've even got false lashes on.

You haven't clocked me yet, which is merciful as my mouth is full of sausage roll and I'm dusted with pastry, but you rush over to Marg.

I can't help smiling as I swallow. To say you've made an effort is an understatement.

Now, the party's started.

Even Nigel's noticed you. I catch him looking. He raises his eyebrows, impressed. He'd probably wolf whistle if he could get away with it.

The guy from the FILTH café comes over for a chat with his wife. It turns out they're from Greenwich, where I lived for a while, years ago. We start talking about London versus Hastings – a favourite FILTH talking point, but I notice you glancing at me from across the room, and eventually, I break free and head your way.

I kiss you on the cheek, compliment how good you look, check you have a drink.

'This place is gorgeous, Bob!' you enthuse. 'I didn't realise Hastings needed a cute... What is this, candle shop? But now I see it, I don't know how we ever survived without one.'

I laugh. 'We sell crystals too. And dreamcatchers!'

'Oh, fabulous! I'll know where to come for all my rose quartz needs.'

You have a cheeky look in your eye. And I like your teasing. I like it a lot.

You eye me over the rim of your glass. Everything about you is perfect, except for that damn locket still hanging around your neck.

'We do jewellery too,' I comment, clumsily trying to segue into asking you about it. 'I like your necklace,' I add, as though it's just a casual observation.

You reach for it, glance down, as though you've forgotten you even had it on.

'Oh, thank you.'

I clear my throat. 'Is it... a tribute to Nathaniel?' I ask, keeping my voice breezy. Not rattled, not at all.

If you tell me it has his ashes in it or some shit, I honestly don't know what I'll do.

'Oh, no!' You laugh. 'It was a gift for my daughter Cara's christening. It's got her baby picture inside. I don't know, I've just felt like wearing it recently. It's been a hard time for her. I think I want to keep her close.'

I smile, totally relieved.

'That's beautiful,' I say, my voice full of compassion, tenderness.

You mirror my smile, eyes twinkling.

'Look...' You fiddle with it, snapping it open to reveal a faded shot of Cara's chubby baby face.

'Oh wow!' I exclaim. 'She's so cute!'

I might be overdoing it, but your locket has nothing to do with Nathaniel, and I am drinking.

'Thanks!' You blush.

You blush.

You snap your locket closed again, and Nigel, who's heading to the drinks table, does a cheeky wink at me over your shoulder.

I try to think of something else to say to you, when Marg appears.

'Lovely party, Bob. Lovely.'

She's sozzled. Her eyes are glassy and she's jerkily brandishing a glass of prosecco.

'Glad you're having a nice time, Marg!'

'I am, but not as much as you two.' She winks. It's a laborious, awkward wink. A touch too slow.

You smirk.

'You two have a little spark, don't you?' Marg smiles conspiratorially.

I laugh, awkwardly this time. What the hell? I thought I was playing it cool. I had no idea anyone could sense a thing.

'You do, don't you?' Marg insists, a bit louder.

I'm almost embarrassed to look you in the eye, but you're smiling, bashfully, as though you've been rumbled.

You feel it. You feel something for me!

'Come on Marg,' you say, cupping her arm. 'Let's get you a vol-au-vent.'

I laugh. You steer Marg away, smiling back at me.

'I think it would be lovely, you two. Finding happiness in each other after such pain,' Marg says as you lead her off.

You get Marg a plate of food from the buffet table and glance over at me, your cheeks slightly pink, and I feel alive. Completely and utterly alive, for the first time in God knows how long.

I work the room, not wanting to come on too strong. I only want to talk to you, but I try to maintain a semblance of normalcy.

Weirdly, I find I'm enjoying myself. I'm enjoying talking to people, laughing, having jokes and banter, feeling the energy in the room, seeing my shop back, thriving once more. It's the best night I've had in a long time, a very long time, and I can barely believe it's real and not just a dream, a figment of my imagination. Only a few months ago, I was a shell of a person, invisible to all, a nonentity. And now here I am, at the centre of a party. *My* party. A party where everyone is having a good time.

I feel a tap on my arm, and it's you.

You're smiling, flushed.

'I've had such a great night, Bob!'

You hug me. You're tipsy.

But you hug me. A tight hug. A real hug.

You smell like washing powder and cheap perfume, and I don't want to let go.

'Sorry if this is weird,' you say, up close, into my ear. 'I've just had such a nice night.'

You pull away.

'Come back.'

You raise an eyebrow.

I catch myself, laugh.

'I mean to the shop. Come back. Bring Cara! She can pick something she wants, anything. On the house, of course.'

Your eyes light up. You like that idea.

'She'd love that!'

'Great. Come along then, any time.'

'Okay then, I'll do that.'

'Brilliant.'

I give you another hug, for a beat longer than the last one.

You bat your lashes as you walk away, promising to see me soon, waving over your shoulder. And I smile. At you, at the world, at life.

Chapter Twenty-Three

Five days pass without you visiting the shop and I'm beginning to wonder if you're going to come at all.

Five days...

Was it just the prosecco that made you keen? Have you decided that, actually, it's too soon for you to entertain the idea of seeing someone new? Maybe you got carried away, had fun flirting for the first time in years, but deep down I'm nothing to you.

I serve customers, put on a smile, and I have moments when I feel like I've stepped back in time, and life is just like the old days. I exist again, and I'm still high on it. I can still barely believe it.

Weirdly, I stop thinking about spirituality, the bigger picture. I stop meditating, stop reading all those books, those strange spiritual texts. I abandon *The Upanishads* and I stop listening to *The Rising Sun Show* podcast quite so much. I stop craving Serena Soulful's wisdom. It's like I've zoomed back into my life after having zoomed out for a very long time. I'm plugged into my day-to-day life again, enjoying the little things.

I take pleasure in dressing up in my old effete way, all mussed up hair, glasses, blazers. Peacocking a bit if I feel like it with whacky shirts, sometimes even nail polish. I'm a regular once more at The Albion. I feel like I've got mates. I don't need to transcend anymore.

Maybe I could be happy without you. Maybe it'll be fine if you don't come into the shop. And yet, I'm not ready to let the fantasy go. Things are better now, much better, but there's still something missing. I know you belong in this new, old life of mine, Natalie. I know you do.

But then, five days turn into six, and then seven, and you've barely given anything away on Facebook, and I'm starting to lose hope.

And then, on day eight, you appear.

You waft in, clasping Cara's hand.

I grin and wave, totally forgetting to play it cool. But you smile back, widely, matching my enthusiasm. Cara lets go of your hand and starts running around the shop. She's immediately drawn to the snow globes. Little girls always love them.

I want to approach you, maybe kiss you on the cheek, but I'm busy wrapping up some soap for a customer. You rifle through a rail of hippy clothes, pick up one of the bucket hats from my old stock.

Cara hasn't looked my way yet, but her presence makes me kind of nervous.

Children always unnerve me.

They're insightful, intuitive, smart. Less blunted than adults, most of whom have calcified their pineal glands beyond repair.

As I wrap the soap, commenting to the customer on what a nice choice it is, I'm hit with a horrible fear that Cara might recognise me. That she might run up to me any second now and exclaim, 'that's the delivery man!'

And then you'll somehow piece everything together and realise I'm a stalkerish, disgraceful creep and not this raffish, ramshackle Mr Charming after all.

I hand the customer her bagged up soap and she leaves, and then it's just the three of us in the shop and my heart's beating heavily and fast.

'Mummy, look at this!' Cara brandishes a dreamcatcher at you.

'Put that down, honey. Don't break it.' You look my way as you take the dreamcatcher from Cara. 'Sorry!' you say.

Cara follows your gaze, her eyes landing on me. Nothing, absolutely no recognition whatsoever passes over her face. I'm a stranger to her.

Relief washes over me. My heartrate steadies.

'She can have it if she likes,' I suggest brightly, coming over to you, glancing at the dreamcatcher in your hand.

Cara looks at me like I'm Santa.

'Mummy!'

'Really?' you ask, unsure.

'Of course!'

'Wow, thanks Bob. That's so kind.' You crouch down to Cara. 'Would you like this, sweetheart?'

'Yes please, mummy!'

'Okay then! Say thanks to Bob.'

Cara looks up at me.

'Thanks Bob!' she says shyly, cutely.

We laugh.

'She seems happy,' I comment as Cara holds up the dreamcatcher, twirling it.

'Yeah, she does. She's doing a lot better,' you say, which is obvious. Cara's like a normal kid now – bright, excitable, engaged. I think of her crying at Beachy Head. The way Nathaniel manhandled her into the car.

But I just nod, and say, 'That's fantastic'.

On a whim, I ask what you're doing now and suggest we go for a walk along the beach. It's a bright, nice day.

'Oh!' You hesitate, and I wonder if I've overstepped the mark. Perhaps you're on your way somewhere. Perhaps you only wanted to treat Cara and I'm taking things too far.

'Sure, that would be nice.'

'Excellent! I'll lock up.'

I take the sign in from outside, reminding myself to play it cool, while you inspect gemstones with Cara. I put on my coat, switch off the lights.

As we're leaving, I grab a chunk of fool's gold.

'Hey Cara, want some gold?'

I hand it to her, and she's delighted.

We head outside.

Cara skips down the street, overjoyed.

'I'm a millionaire! I'm a millionaire!' she exclaims to no one in particular.

I smile. No one would know her father had just died. No one in a million years.

'That was nice of you Bob,' you say, sweetly.

'It's nothing.'

I ask how you're doing.

'I'm up and down,' you tell me, tucking your hair back behind your ear. You're wearing dangling earrings, ruby red lipstick. There's colour in your cheeks and you look very Snow White today, up close under the wintry sky.

'That's understandable. Grief's a journey, right? Like Sandra says.'

'Yeah, exactly. Something like that.' You smile sadly. A bit too sadly in my opinion. 'What about you? How are you holding up?'

'Oh, I'm fine. I love having my shop open again. It's just a little shop, but it makes me happy, you know?'

'Of course, yeah. I meant...' You frown.

You meant my mother. My dead mother. Who I completely fucking forgot about.

Fuck.

'I'm kind of struggling to talk about my mum at the moment. Maybe I'm repressing it or something.'

'Oh, right. Yeah, that makes sense.' You smile tentatively, sympathetically.

I think I've just about covered my tracks. For God's sake though.

Conversation flows more freely as we make our way to the promenade. Seagulls squawk and swoop as I look out to sea.

'Your mum would be proud of you, Bob,' you say. 'With the shop and all.'

My heart quivers. Your voice is so gentle, so kind. Tears prick my eyes, although I'm not sure why. Maybe it's the sea breeze. Maybe it's the fact that my mother's alive, in Slough, and she couldn't care less. Never has and never will. But I can't tell you that. I could never tell you that.

You take my hand. Squeeze it.

You're touching me. I turn to you.

Your eyes are deep, more oceanic than the ocean, and everything beyond falls away. I squeeze your hand, lace my fingers through yours, and you don't let go.

I hope you'll never let go.

CHAPTER TWENTY-FOUR

We're texting.

'Let's stay in touch,' you said at the end of our walk along the promenade, getting your phone from your bag.

You were keen, and it's not like I objected.

I couldn't type your digits in quick enough.

We message about all sorts. Day-to-day stuff. What you're up to – spending a lot of quality time with Cara and your mum, mainly. Your nursing dreams. Funny customers in the shop. Our pasts. You, born and bred here, having attended The Saint Leonards Academy before nursing school. A lot of the stuff you tell me, I already know, but obviously I don't let that show. I give you a sanitized version of my own upbringing.

I reveal that it was pretty working class, and yet I make it sound hearty and character-building, rather than soul-destroying and grim. I scrape the bottom of the barrel for good qualities about my parents and tell you those. It helps that my family are dying off (I'll 'kill' off dad sometime soon), so you'll never actually meet them.

Maybe I should feel bad for twisting the truth, but it's not like I'm the only one.

You gloss over your relationship with Nathaniel, hiding what he was really like. The closest you get is saying your relationship was 'hard work', which is hardly revealing. Most relationships are hard work, but most men aren't Nathaniel.

It would be nice if you opened up a bit, trusted me. But it is early days, and I guess it's understandable that you'd be guarded after what he did to you.

I want to show you that life can be good. That you can trust people and be happy and shine that beautiful light of yours far and wide.

I want you to finish that nursing course. Follow your dreams.

We talk about jobs at the local hospital. You say you're looking into it. You're focusing on Cara and then you'll apply. I believe you.

You ask about my work history. I tell you about some of the jobs I've had over the years. I leave out the courier stuff, but I tell you about some of the odd jobs: working as a handyman, my stint as a wannabe artist. I make a lot of self-effacing jokes, which you seem to find amusing.

The weekend's coming up and I need to see you.

I suggest dinner. A new Malaysian place in Saint Leonards that looks classy enough.

You're game.

We don't call it a date, but I'm pretty sure we both know that that's what it is. I even buy a new blazer. Well, a second-hand one: vintage Versace from one of the thrift shops on George Street. And I get a haircut. Nothing too extreme, but a flattering tidy-up.

I buy you flowers. I can't resist. I want to get a dozen red roses, but that would be too much, so I settle for one of those pretty, wintry bouquets instead.

As I stand outside the restaurant, in my Versace blazer, hair artfully preened, clutching the bouquet and wearing aftershave for the first time in years, I feel about as vulnerable as I can physically tolerate. I half-want to jump in a passing taxi and head home, just to save myself the emotional rawness of this moment, and then, you show up. And if I thought your Christmas fairy look was nice, well tonight... Tonight you've really pulled out all the stops.

You're head-to-toe in black. Short velvet dress, leather jacket, pointed stilettos, heavy eyeliner and smoky eyes. You look like a singer in a band.

'Wow,' I gasp, taking you in, kissing you on the cheek. You smell delicious. 'You look incredible!'

'Thanks!' You look me up and down. 'You look pretty good too.'

I'll take it.

We head inside. I catch our reflection in a gilded mirror. We look good together, attractive, richer than we are.

The waitress shows us to our table, which I'm pleased to see is flickering with tealights.

We order a bottle of wine and a selection of dishes, and pick up where we left off in our messages. Cara. The shop. Chit-chat.

And then we delve into deeper topics.

You want to know more. You want to know about my university days, and London.

I tell you about my degree, trying to be humble. I doubt you know that many people who went to Durham.

'So is it good for English, then?' You say, topping up our glasses.

I smile through gritted teeth.

Usually, people know Durham's good. Saying you went there means something. You don't even seem to know that it's a decent university! But my irritation isn't anything a glass of wine can't flush away.

'Yes, it's pretty good,' I tell you.

You nod.

'I wish I had more time to read, but I only really manage to get through magazines with Cara running around,' you say sheepishly.

I suppose at least you think I'm learned, sophisticated. I guess that's something.

'You can read all the books in the world and still not be interesting. Life is about experience,' I tell you, not really sure I believe it.

154

You seem to like the sentiment, though.

'You're so right,' you say emphatically, taking a bite of your laksa curry.

You look captivating in the candlelight.

We compare meals, tasting each other's dishes. Appraise the place.

'I think this one might last,' you muse.

I laugh at that.

I know exactly what you mean. Both of us are attuned to passing FILTH businesses and we compare notes.

'Remember the vegan dog grooming parlour?'

'Or that café where you got to paint your own cup?'

We laugh a lot and order more wine. Your laugh is surprisingly loud, and a bit low, and you clasp your hand to your chest when you really go for it.

You're funny. Different. Better company than I even imagined.

By the time we move on to dessert, we're talking about travel. Well, it starts with Saint Leonards versus Brighton, and then we get further afield. You tell me about your family holidays in Tenerife.

I decide not to mention that I've been to every continent and lost track of how many countries.

To my surprise, you mention Everest. How you'd love to climb it and that you're hoping you can get up to Edinburgh at some point, explore the Highlands.

I stare at you, perplexed, and then I realise you think Everest is in Scotland.

'I've always wanted to climb the mountains there. What is it they call it? Monroe-bagging?'

'I think so,' I squeak. 'Sorry, excuse me a moment.'

I rush to the gents, stash myself in a cubicle, and fucking guffaw. I have to bite my fist to stop myself from laughing.

Everest. In Scotland!

I can't believe it. I cannot wait to tell Nigel.

Eventually, I calm down, sort myself out. Make sure my face is serious and respectful in the mirror.

After all, it's not your fault you haven't travelled. That you haven't been properly educated. I can work with this.

You're like a blank canvas. We can explore together. I can see the world afresh through your eyes or something. It's not like I chose you for your intellect.

And if I'm totally honest, I kind of like that you're not on my level. Nothing's worse than dating someone with shrewd eyes, an analytical mind. No, I want to be with someone like you. Someone who thinks Everest is in Scotland. It gives me a sense of peace and privacy to know that certain things go over your head.

You're good and pure and straightforward. Whereas I'm murky and bad and complicated. You're the yin to my yang; it makes us work.

I've gone for clever women before, insightful women, and look where it's got me? Never again. I want *you* now.

I emerge from the toilets, feeling calmer.

You look sweet, almost childlike, sitting at the table on your own, finishing your sorbet.

We polish off the wine and I pick up the bill.

Pretty pissed, we stumble out onto the street.

Staggering on your heels, you grab my arm for support.

'Fancy a walk?' you ask.

'Are you sure? In those?' I glance down at your shoes.

'I'll take them off. Let's go to the beach.'

I shrug. 'Okay.'

So we head down to the sea.

The sky's black, the ocean's silver and the moon glows as we crunch over pebbles. It's too cold for you to take off your stilettos, and so you're tottering along, gripping me tightly for support.

I turn to you. Your eyes are dark and deep in the moonlight.

My heart swells as your hair blows across your face, buffeted by the sea breeze.

I reach towards you, sweep it away, and lean in to kiss you.

Our lips meet. Tentative at first, soft, and then your tongue finds mine. You pull me close. I kiss you passionately, my hands in your hair and you kiss me passionately back, and this is everything,

everything, I thought it would be, and so much more.

To say we've had a good date would be an understatement.

CHAPTER TWENTY-FIVE

The following week, you go quiet.

You don't reply to my messages. Not for two whole days, which is a long time for us at this point. And then, in the evening, you call.

'Bob.' You sound a bit breathless, panicked. 'Sorry, I've been AWOL. I think it's the grief or something. I don't know... I've felt a bit flaky. What are you doing?'

You're unhinged, and I like it.

I think in a way, you do, too. You can be a bit wilder now you're grieving, a bit freer. You can do things and say things you might not have done or said before, and if anyone questions you, you can blame Nathaniel.

'I'm at home!' I tell you. 'Just had dinner.'

I had been planning to meditate since the lack of messages had got me feeling strung out. I don't tell you that though.

'I know it's late and out of the blue and everything, but is there any way you could come over? Just for a bit. Cara's at my mum's. I don't know... For some reason, I don't want to be alone tonight.'

'Sure,' I say, not skipping a beat.

Fifteen minutes later, I'm pulling up outside your house. First time I've been here in my new car, my Renault.

It's kind of awkward to be at your house again, but I knew this was going to happen eventually.

As I get out of the car, I'm almost nervous one of the neighbours might shout out of their window – 'Look! It's that courier who was poking around the night Nathaniel died!'

But no one says a thing and I remind myself that no one notices couriers. And no one would recognise me in a million years anyway.

You open the front door. You look cute. Low-key in loungewear, with light make-up, your hair in that messy side plait.

You kiss me and pull me inside.

'Thanks for coming,' you say, leading me into the sitting room, where you flop onto the sofa. 'I guess you found it okay?'

'Yeah, wasn't too hard,' I comment. 'It's not far.'

I notice a bottle of red on the coffee table, a bowl of crisps, even dip.

'Decided to make a bit of an effort. It's not much, but...'

'You're lovely,' I say, grateful for the prospect of a glass of wine after my fairly manic dash here.

You pour me a glass.

'I'm on the lemonade.' You glance at your own sparkling glass. 'Still kind of recovering from our date the other day!'

I laugh.

You're sitting where Nathaniel sat, and my mind flashes back to his limp body, plunging the syringe into his arm, the tourniquet.

'You okay?' you ask, perplexed, and I realise I must look strange.

I correct my expression as best I can, but I feel out of sorts. Being here is freaking me out more than I thought it would.

'You seem a bit... I don't know... off. You look pale.'

I take a hungry sip of wine, assure you I'm fine.

'I think I've got a cold coming on or something.' I shrug, chugging at my glass.

'Oh, okay.'

You snuggle into me.

'I've missed you,' you say. 'It's good to see you again.'

We kiss, once more. Longer this time.

'I've missed you too,' I tell you.

'I feel like you're the only person who understands me right now. You understand grief, you know?'

'Mmm,' I murmur.

I hate it when you talk about Nathaniel dying. You didn't even mention him on our date. Why now?

'There's just something different about you. Something gentle, sensitive. I feel I can be myself around you.'

I smile. That's better.

You go on about your feelings for a while. The good days, the bad days. The dreams you've been having.

I find myself drinking quite a lot, because no offence Natalie, but there's nothing more boring than listening to someone else's nonsensical dreams.

Then you start talking about the guilt you feel at moving on, and finding me, and my ears prick up.

'Love just happens. You can't schedule it,' I comment. Kind of poetic, actually.

Your eyes go wide and then it hits me. I said 'love'. *Love.* Holy fuck! We've been on one fucking date.

'I mean theoretically. Love just happens. Obviously, we're not there yet. But we feel something for each other, that spark, and you—'

You shut me up with a kiss, clambering on top of me.

I thought the kiss we had at the beach was passionate, but this is different. This is entirely different. You're fervent, hungry.

You grind against me. You're hot, horny. You want to fuck.

It's early, Natalie. Is this the grief talking again, your unhinged side? Should we really be doing this or is it too soon? I don't want you to use me. And yet, my dick's rock solid, my breathing shallow, and my hands are creeping under your top, feeling your stiff little nipples, and I know we're going to fuck. No two ways about it.

I slip my hand inside your jogging bottoms. You're not wearing any underwear and your soft pussy is warm and slick.

I slide my fingers into you. You moan.

You wriggle out of your bottoms and toss them aside, before freeing my bulging cock from my jeans, and then you mount me, moaning as you push down onto my dick.

You're wilder than I thought you'd be, and I like it.

Your eyes are black with desire, and you grind onto me. Groaning, moaning, your hands in my hair. You're frenzied, ravenous. I reach under your top again, squeeze your tits. Your body's hot, beading with sweat as you ride me.

I lose myself in the wildness, unable to contain animal groans as I match your thrusts, pounding into you.

I still can't quite believe we're fucking!

I have a fleeting thought of Nathaniel. In a weird way, I feel slightly watched, but fuck it, he can enjoy the show.

I consider flipping you over, doing you from behind. I've imagined it enough times, but I feel kind of sleepy, lazy. Maybe it's the wine. You seem to be enjoying yourself, anyway. You seem to quite like taking the lead.

'Oh, Natalie,' I groan, grabbing your ass as you jerk up and down my dick. 'Oh, baby.'

'Oh yes. Yes. Fuck!' you cry out, grinding, moaning. You tug at my hair, gasping. Your pussy gets tighter, contracts, and you hold me tight, rubbing your clit against me, back and forth, and you come, convulsing, crying out blasphemies, gasping.

Your orgasm sets me off and, well... Well, I fucking explode.

I come so hard it's like my brain obliterates for a moment, bursting into infinite galaxies, and I'm just pure fucking *pleasure*.

It's glorious.

'Wow...' I come back to reality and catch my breath.

You pull yourself off my cock and slump next to me.

'Yeah, wow. I needed that,' you say, a little gruffly.

I raise an eyebrow, smile. Your orgasm's really loosened you up.

'I have to say, your cock's quite a lot bigger than Nathaniel's. I had a feeling it might be. I don't know, a sixth sense or something. A woman's intuition!'

I laugh awkwardly. *What the fuck?*

You get up. The baggy top you're wearing just about covers your pussy.

You wander over to the mirror above the mantlepiece, check your reflection.

'Thanks, by the way,' you say, as you adjust your hair.

Another awkward laugh. 'You don't have to thank me.'

You roll your eyes in the mirror.

'I don't mean for the sex.'

You turn to me, a weird, smirking expression on your face.

'What do you mean?'

You laugh. Your eyes are penetrating, jarring.

'What you did...'

The hairs on the back of my neck stand up.

'Excuse me?'

'Oh, come on, Bob. I know.'

'Know what?'

'You don't seriously think I didn't notice your van, do you? Do you really think I didn't see it, parked at the end of the road all the time? I was always at home, I had nothing better to do than to spy on the neighbours, keep an eye on the street. I saw you driving by, parking up, watching.'

I feel slightly dizzy and reach for my wine.

'Do you really think taking off a pair of sunglasses and a hat makes you look like a new man?' you scoff. 'I know you did our deliveries. You saw me and Cara that day, looking desperate. I was hoping someone would notice us. The number of times I tried to get the attention of postmen, Uber Eats drivers, delivery guys like you. I wanted somebody to see we were being abused, raise the alarm, do something. I knew if I told anyone we knew, Nathaniel would fucking destroy me. And then you took notice. Finally.'

I gawp at you. Is this really happening? This cannot be happening.

'You're Dan Reid, right? My new Facebook friend. Next time you might want to use a VPN because I traced your IP address. Wasn't exactly in Hackney! And that profile was clearly fake! Piece of advice: never join MI6.'

Who the fuck are you?

'Do you know what? I thought you'd beat Nathaniel up or report him. Maybe you'd even gather some evidence, I don't know. I thought you'd help somehow... I tried to end him myself at one point. Persuaded him to take us for a walk at

Beachy Head, even tried to push him off. I know, mad, right? He went *ballistic*. But, of course, you know that. You were there.'

I knock back my wine. I can barely look at you. My heart's racing. Everything feels strange, surreal, overwhelming, like I'm not really here.

'I was hoping you'd do *something*, but I didn't expect you to actually kill him! That was insane! Pretty clever. The police fell for it hook, line and sinker. I knew it was fake, though. Nathaniel would never have done drugs again. *We* were his outlet, his way of letting off steam. Me and Cara.'

You glance at the floor, a shadow passing over your face.

'And the whole thing was a bit staged. A bit fake. The speed in the drawer was a real giveaway. Nathaniel never touched speed, even at the peak of his druggie days. *Hated* the stuff. Said it made him paranoid. I couldn't get my head around it all at first, and then I found your hat out the back and I realised what you'd done.'

You laugh. 'Your face, Bob! You should see yourself! Don't worry, I binned the hat. No one knows. I mean, you did do me a favour.'

'What the fuck...' I mutter, almost to myself. I don't know if it's the panic or what, but I really do feel completely removed from myself, like I'm drowning, slipping away.

'For someone educated at Durham, I'd have expected something a little more sophisticated to be honest. I mean, you even drove your creepy delivery van to the support group meeting! That was a bit sloppy. Hardly subtle. I was parked in the corner of the car park. You didn't see me. I was sitting in my car, not wanting to go in. I only went along because my mum thought I should go. I'd been sitting there, about to go home, and then I saw you. I couldn't believe it! Thought I'd go in and see what the hell you were doing there.'

You shake your head.

'Honestly, Bob,' you tut. 'Grooming someone at a grief support group. Classy! All those pervy looks you were giving me. And did you really think I fell for your sob story? No one has a party when they're grieving!'

'I can't believe this...'

'I know, I know. You thought I was a dipshit, a bimbo, a small-town nobody. You thought the longest thing I'd ever read was a bumper edition of Cosmo. I get it!' you sneer. 'Oh, and for the record, I know Everest isn't in fucking Scotland! Your face when I said that!'

'You're a liar,' I spit. 'You're a fucking liar.'

'Oops! Busted! I mean, you're not exactly squeaky clean yourself, Bob.'

'I loved you...'

You snort. 'You don't know what love is! You know, if you'd gone about this normally... If you'd reported Nathaniel, introduced yourself, behaved like a decent, regular human being, I might genuinely have liked you. We might have had something. You're not totally repellent, you know. You have some charm. But instead, you thought you'd be a weird, sneaky creep. You thought you'd murder a man and manipulate everyone.'

I've had enough. Fuck this. Fuck you.

'You bitch.'

I move, wanting to lunge towards you and smash your face against that mirror, except my legs won't budge. They're stiff, really stiff, heavy beyond belief. In fact, my whole body feels kind of *leaden.*

'Ketamine,' you say. 'Laced the wine. You've had quite a lot.'

'What the fuck?' I try to get up, but my body won't comply. I can't seem to lift myself from this fucking sofa.

'You're not the only one with access to drugs, you know.'

You turn, open a box on the mantlepiece, and retrieve a syringe.

I watch in horror. My body's limp, I can't get away. I look to the door, wanting escape, pining for it. I desperately, *desperately*, try to get up as you approach me, syringe bared.

'Natalie, no...'

I try to reach up to stop you, but you stand over me. My arms are floppy, I can't quite reach up.

'Karma.' You shrug.

And then I feel a prick on my neck, and everything goes black.

ABOUT THE
AUTHOR

Zoe Rosi is a thriller author based in the UK. She has written two full-length thrillers, *Pretty Evil* and *Someone's Watching Me*.

Pretty Evil was first released in 2020 at the height of MeToo and features a vigilante killer of predatory men. Zoe describes the novel as '*The*

Devil Wears Prada meets *American Psycho*'. Zoe's second thriller, *Someone's Watching Me*, is a gritty psychological suspense that deals with themes of stalking and gaslighting.

Courier is Zoe's first novella. She had the idea for the book after wondering what would happen if a courier developed an obsession with one of the people they delivered to. We all use couriers these days, more so now than ever, and we barely give it a second thought, but what if this easy everyday convenience suddenly became toxic? This is the thought that gave birth to Bob.

If you enjoyed *Courier*, please consider leaving a review online.

To find out more about Zoe's books, visit her website at www.zoerosi.com or follow her on social media, where she is @zoerosiauthor on both Twitter and Instagram.

Printed in Great Britain
by Amazon

45095194R00099